Praise for *Bitter Sweets*, shortlisted for the
Orange Award for New Writers 2007

'Witty, thought-provoking, sad and uplifting'
Sunday Telegraph

'Roopa Farooki is already being called the next Zadie
Smith. But *Bitter Sweets* is so thoroughly absorbing that
Farooki proves she needs no comparison. *Bitter Sweets* is
a piercing examination of the blurry lines between love and
desire, truth and self-protection and guilt and redemption.
Farooki tells a vivid, unforgettable story'   *BookPage* (US)

'[A] fizzy debut novel . . . Ms Farooki creates the strong
suspicion that she could tell a story about any type of
people. Despite its emphasis on deception, dislocation and
the loss of love, her book retains a cheery consistency: it
has managed to be sunnily devious from the start. And it
delivers a refreshing message'   *New York Times*

'Combining the cultural heritage of Monica Ali's *Brick
Lane* with the intimate humour of family life in Roddy
Doyle's novels, Farooki explores complex and sensitive
issues of ethnic difference, the values of family, and atti-
tudes to relationships in an enlightening and tender way'
Easy Living

'Charming . . . hugely enjoyable, brilliantly plotted'
Jackie Kay, Chair of Orange Award for New Writers 2007

Praise for *Corner Shop*

'*Corner Shop* is really magnificent . . . I couldn't put it down. You have to read this book'
                                                    Nikki Bedi, BBC Asian Network

'This delightful, wise novel is about the dangers waiting for people who pursue their dreams. Farooki manages the emotional minefield with humour and compassion'
                                                    The Times

'Aspirations and family ties play out across three generations of the Khalil family in Farooki's fine new novel. This character- and culture-rich novel will appeal to Jhumpa Lahiri and Zadie Smith fans'
                                                    Publishing Weekly (US)

'Farooki writes tales of multicultural, contemporary Britain populated by funny, believable characters – full of flaws, compassion and humanity'   *Financial Times*

'A complex exploration of the ever-changing nature of wants and desires and the consequences of achieving one's dreams, Farooki's tale eschews easy answers for the complex, appealing characters that people its pages'
                                                    Booklist (US)

Praise for *The Way Things Look to Me*,
one of *The Times* Top 50 Paperbacks of 2009

'Characters so nuanced, flawed and engaging, they virtually jump off the page ... this novel is a treat ... the narratives swirl around each other in this warm, wonderful portrait of a charmingly atypical family' *Easy Living*

'A tender-hearted novel that examines how siblings keep one another afloat. A writer with few pretensions, Farooki is happy to tell it how it is'   *Independent*

'Superbly uplifting. Heartwarming to the core'
                                                    Cosmopolitan

'Farooki has such a firm grasp of character and plot that she succeeds in telling a story that is engaging and convincing to the end ... she makes everything count in a tale that combines familial dysfunction with an honest appraisal of personal disability. It is an important book ... Roopa Farooki knows how to write'
                                                Action for Autism

'Both humorous and poignant. While there are a few novels around that feature characters on the autistic spectrum, this one breaks new ground. A perceptive novel'   *Waterstone's Books Quarterly*

'A beautifully written book. Five Stars'   *Grazia*

Roopa Farooki was born in Lahore in Pakistan and brought up in London. She graduated from New College, Oxford and worked in advertising before turning to write fiction. Roopa now lives in south-east England and south-west France with her husband, twin baby girls and two sons and teaches creative writing on the MA programme at Canterbury Christ Church University. *Bitter Sweets*, her first novel, was shortlisted for the Orange Award for New Writers 2007. Her next novel, *Corner Shop*, was published to critical acclaim in several countries, and her third novel, *The Way Things Look to Me*, was selected by *The Times* as one of the top 50 paperbacks of 2009.

www.roopafarooki.com

For David
All best wishes ♡Roopa x

Half Life

Roopa Farooki

MACMILLAN

First published 2010 by Macmillan
an imprint of Pan Macmillan, a division of Macmillan Publishers Limited
20 New Wharf Road, London N1 9RR
Basingstoke and Oxford
Associated companies throughout the world
www.panmacmillan.com

ISBN 978-0-230-74585-8

1 3 5 7 9 8 6 4 2

A CIP catalogue record for this book is available from
the British Library.

Typset by SetSystems Ltd, Saffron Walden, Essex
Printed in Great Britain by CPI Mackays, Chatham ME5 8TD

Visit **www.panmacmillan.com** to read more about all our books
and to buy them. You will also find features, author interviews and
news of any author events, and you can sign up for e-newsletters
so that you're always first to hear about our new releases.

For my mother, Niluffer Farooki,
with gratitude and love

I measure every grief I meet
   With analytic eyes;
I wonder if it weighs like mine
   Or has an easier size . . .

The grieved are many, I am told;
   There is the various cause;
Death is but one and comes but once
   And only nails the eyes.

Emily Dickinson

Since I left you, mine eye is in my mind . . .

For if it see the rudest or gentlest sight,
The most sweet favour or deformed'st creature,
The mountain or the sea, the day or night,
The crow or dove, it shapes them to your feature:
      Incapable of more, replete with you,
      My most true mind thus makes mine eye untrue.

William Shakespeare, Sonnet CXIII

Aruna

King Edward's Road, Bethnal Green, London

It's time to stop fighting, and go home. Those were the words which finally persuaded Aruna to walk out of her ground-floor Victorian flat in Bethnal Green, and keep on walking. One step at a time, one foot, and then the other, her inappropriately flimsy sandals flip-flopping on the damp east London streets; she avoids the dank, brown puddles, the foil glint of the takeaway containers glistening with the vibrant slime of sweet and sour sauce, the mottled banana skin left on the pavement like a practical joke, but otherwise walks in a straight line. One foot, and then the other. Toe to heel to toe to heel. Flip-flop. She knows exactly where she is going, and even though she could have carried everything she needs in her dressing-gown pocket – her credit card, her passport, her phone – she has taken her handbag instead, and she has paused in her escape long enough to dress in jeans, a T-shirt and even a jacket. Just for show. So that people won't think that she is a madwoman who has walked out on her marriage and her marital home in the middle of breakfast, with her half-eaten porridge congealing in the bowl, with her tea cooling on the counter top. So that she won't think so either. So she can turn up at the airport looking like anyone else, hand over her credit card, and run back to the city she had run away from in the first place.

It's time to stop fighting, and go home. She hasn't left a note. It's not as though she is planning to kill herself, like last time. Then she had left a note, thinking it only polite, to exonerate her husband from any blame or self-reproach, to apologize and excuse herself, as though she were a schoolgirl asking to be let off gym class, instead of the rest of her life. When she had returned, having not gone through with it after all, her hair damp and reedy-smelling, as though she had simply been swimming in the Hampstead Heath Ponds instead of trying to drown herself there, the note was still on the counter. Patrick had been working late. She wasn't sure if she had failed to end her life because she was too lazy and non-committal – she hadn't tried hard enough; the gentle, shallow water hadn't tried hard enough either, it had bobbed her back up again and offered no helpful current. Perhaps, like the water, she was just too kind – it was kinder for everyone if she lived, wasn't it? All life, even a life as unimportant as hers, performed some kindness to those it touched; wouldn't her husband, if no one else, appreciate this kindness? Or perhaps that was just vanity – she hadn't destroyed the note, but had smoothed it into their diary on the kitchen table, as one might a shopping list, or a love letter, or a poem; but Patrick had never noticed it, because he didn't make appointments, she supposed. She eventually screwed it up and put it into the recycling box, which Patrick did take care of, judiciously separating paper, glass and plastic. He still didn't see it – or if he did, he saw it as just another piece of paper. Patrick, ironically for a medical professional whose job is to observe, seems to see very little indeed, at least when it comes to her. He persistently mistakes her for someone better than she is, as though his gaze stops just short of her. He frequently expresses his love for her, but the truth is that he doesn't know her very well, and she is sure that should he need to fill out a missing persons form, he would be distressed to realize that he doesn't know her height, her weight, her dress size. He would possibly even be unsure of her exact age and birthday. Although he would probably get her hair and eyes right, as she has the same hair and eyes as almost every woman of Bengali descent. She imagines him filling out this part of the form with confidence, with relief, even; hair: black, eyes: brown.

She didn't leave a note this time, as she has no idea what she would have put in it; apart from saying that she had left, but her absence would do this anyway. Wouldn't it? Was it possible that Patrick would come home and go to work and come home and go to work and not notice until the weekend that she was missing, assuming that she was out shopping or working late in the faculty library, especially as she has recently been in the business of avoiding him in order to steer clear of the difficult conversation about babies that he seems so intent on pursuing. Was she wrong in assuming that her absence would be more noticeable than her presence? They live parallel, independent lives, and have always done so; he complains that even when she's in, she's out. When at home she supposes that she is not much more than a small creature curled indifferently on the sofa or in the bath or in the corner of the bed, scrawling in her notebooks with a quiet persistent scratching, working on her laptop with a quiet persistent tapping, but otherwise barely there, without a height or a weight or a dress size worth recalling.

She supposes that such a note should say the truth about why she is leaving, but there is no larger truth. There is nothing significant. There is no Big Important Question to be answered. She has not had an affair, she is not in trouble with the law or in debt, she does not hate him or dislike him at all: like most couples, they fight and bicker all the time, about the ridiculous minutiae of their shared life; who last loaded the dishwasher, and where the toilet roll should be stored. They argue about her refusal, thus far, to consider pregnancy and whether to spend Christmas with the in-laws. There is really nothing but the trivial problems of the everyday, and to other people she looks like nothing so much as an ordinary woman, recently married, as yet childless, with ordinary cares. She looks like this even to herself, on occasion; an ordinary woman, in an ordinary life, wondering why she has striven to be ordinary above everything else. Perhaps she expected it would bring her peace of mind, bringing together the pieces of mind that still inhabit her, their little voices whining inside like shards of glass waiting to pierce through her skin and reveal how sliced up and fragmented she has secretly been within herself, for such a long time. The only thing that currently makes her more than ordinary, extraordinary even, is that she has written and recycled a suicide note, without anyone in the world noticing, and that she has decided to stop fighting, and go home.

The funny thing, laugh-out-loud funny when she dwells on it, is that she didn't say those words in an earnest discussion with her husband, they weren't advised her by a mother or a friend or a therapist or a lover. The words simply fell out of a book she had been skim-reading over breakfast that had some relevance to her research; fell out almost as casually as a child's gift from a cereal packet, or junk mail from her morning newspaper. It was a comment between one prodigal son and another, unwilling opponents in a bloody conflict. And as she read it, she thought, OK then. Like a switch had been gently flicked in her head, and she had finally been prompted into action; leaving the breakfast table, dressing carelessly and rather too lightly for the British weather, and taking her handbag. She had put her passport in and taken her keys out, feeling a weight fall from her as she let them tumble onto the glass table in the hall with a musical tinkle. She had breathed a sigh of relief at the sight of them as she shut the door behind her. How easy it was, ridiculously easy, to leave. She suddenly felt so free that she really did laugh out loud, and stopped herself abruptly in case the neighbours heard. It was important to her that she didn't seem mad, that she didn't leave the house in her dressing gown, that she wasn't seen laughing or muttering to herself or crying in the streets; she felt that if she ever let her little bit of insanity out, she might never contain it again, like a wild thing set free. She hadn't laughed because she was mad, she had laughed because some random words written long ago by a stranger had spoken to her, and she had unaccountably given them the importance of a prophecy. Her keys left on the table were her proof – she wouldn't be coming back this time.

Aruna only makes it as far as the cafe on the corner, when she starts to have doubts. It is her reflection in the glass that stops her; she sees herself in her summer jacket and sandals, on a blustery spring day, dressed for the weather of the place she is going to, rather than the place she is leaving. She realizes that although she has dressed, she has not washed her face, brushed her teeth, or combed her hair, which crackles with artless tangles and stands away from her face. She has a feverish flush, and she is sure that she can see that bright glint of madness in her eyes that she has worked so hard to suppress. Her disguise of jeans and a T-shirt isn't working as well as it might – instead of having the invisibility of a Gap ad, she feels as transparently out of place as a bag lady in a ball gown. Perhaps she should have just gone out in her dressing gown after all, because then someone kind would have seen her for what she is, seen her glassy eyes and wild hair, and escorted her back to her flat (not to her home, she never calls the flat home, she just calls it the flat, or occasionally, when she is speaking to American colleagues at her faculty, the apartment). Perhaps this good Samaritan whom she will now never meet, whom she unaccountably regrets not meeting, would have made her a fresh cup of tea, and then tucked her back in bed like an invalid. Her reflection nods at her knowingly – she is acting irresponsibly again. The reflection seems a little too knowing in fact, as though it is no longer connected to her, and imitates her gestures in mockery rather than by necessity; she waves at it tentatively to check that it will wave too. She is taken aback when a figure inside the cafe comes up to the glass, and waves back instead. 'Hi Aruna, nice of you to stop by,' says Syed, the cafe owner, coming across to his open doorway, sipping from a cup of coffee that lets off little wisps of steam into the cool air. Aruna says nothing for a moment, stunned at how easily real life has invaded her again, someone waving to her and naming her, mistakenly thinking that she was greeting them from outside their window. She is unsure whether there is an edge to his voice, a criticism, something that implies she doesn't stop by often enough.

'Hi Sy,' she says eventually, hiding her hostility behind apologetic guilt, as though she really has failed to fulfil some mysterious etiquette regarding the acceptable frequency of attending one's local cafe. Everything makes her feel vaguely on guard, even a casual greeting from a shopkeeper she barely knows.

'Your hubby stopped by this morning too. Picked up his coffee on the way to work. He told me that I was drinking too much of the stuff, can you believe? I said to him, I said, "Patrick, mate, I wouldn't trust a bald hairdresser, I wouldn't trust a skinny chef, and I wouldn't trust a cafe owner who doesn't drink his own coffee."'

Aruna says nothing; her eyes have drifted back to her reflection, and Syed, who is old enough to be her father, asks almost kindly, 'Are you coming in then?' There is no edge to his voice after all, just a touch of impatience, as though she is a dawdling child in need of a little push. Aruna is unable to say no, as that would involve explaining why, and so she nods and drifts in, and takes the seat near the window.

'So, coffee?' suggests Syed, 'I've got the fair trade stuff that you guys like. Americano for you, isn't it?'

'OK,' says Aruna, aware as she says it how ungracious she sounds, as though she is doing him a favour. 'I mean, please.' She sips the coffee when he brings it over, making an appreciative noise at odds with how she really feels.

'And how's the family?' asks Syed politely. Aruna smiles back, just as politely; she has no family, apart from Patrick, and it strikes her as funny that Syed doesn't know this. She is relieved that he doesn't know that much about her after all, perhaps her disguise is still intact.

'Oh, we're all fine. How about yours?' she asks.

'Fine too. My wife went away for the weekend with her girlfriends. Went to Madrid, and complained about how some overpriced restaurant she went to was run by Pakistanis rather than Spaniards. As though we weren't Pakis ourselves. Funny how bigoted she gets when she goes abroad. She expects London to be cosmopolitan but the rest of Europe to be lily white.'

'I didn't know you were from Pakistan,' says Aruna, stirring her coffee.

'Where did you think I was from, with a name like Syed?' he asks.

'I don't know. Here, I guess. I just thought you were English.'

'So, where are you from?' asks Syed, cleaning out the filters, just making conversation. Another couple of customers come in and start examining the chalkboard menu hung on the cafe wall.

'Singapore,' says Aruna, 'But my parents were from the Bengal.' She has another sip of coffee, and realizes that she has to leave, before she gets sucked back into her ordinary life, before she calls a locksmith and gets herself let back into her flat, where she will finish her cold porridge, load the dishwasher (it is her turn, her husband reminded her this morning, trying not to nag, but not quite succeeding) and have a shower. 'I'll leave you to it,' she says, going up to the till and handing over her change.

'Take care. Off to work then?' asks Syed.

'No, I'm going home,' she replies; Syed takes the orders from the new customers, and doesn't notice that Aruna goes in the opposite direction to the place where she lives, and is walking toward the tube station. Flip-flop-flip.

Aruna tries to ignore the curious looks she gets on the Central line train, as suited commuters stare freely at the sandals hanging off her bare feet, at her just-out-of-bed hair, at her obviously bra-less breasts behind her fitted T-shirt. (Why hadn't she remembered to wear a bra? Why didn't she think that underwear mattered just because it couldn't be seen? It seemed that the things which couldn't be seen mattered just as much, if not more.) She scrapes her fingers through her hair until it takes some semblance of order, and then ties it up with an elastic band she finds in her handbag. She puts on lipstick, also found in her handbag, and buttons up her jacket. When she changes for the Piccadilly line at Holborn, she finds that fewer people are staring at her, so she supposes she has succeeded in looking more respectable. She can tell the other travellers going to the airport, not just by their bulky bags, but by their air of not quite belonging; like her, they are no longer dressed like Londoners, they are dressed for their destination too, in sloppy tracksuits for long-haul flights, in hardy shorts with hiking boots, in ethnic shirts with embroidered purses around their necks. Dr Aruna Ahmed Jones, height 5 foot 4 inches, weight 51 kilos, dress size UK 10, age 31 years, birthday June 3rd, hair: black, eyes: brown, pulls out the book she had been reading that morning, the poems and letters of Hari Hassan, a minor but well-reputed Bengali writer. Her paper, which she supposes she will now fail to complete, was to have been about the 'Influences of the Modern Subcontinental Poem'. Hari Hassan had been in the thick of the civil war between East and West Pakistan, from which Bangladesh emerged as a state; in a letter in 1971 he had written to his oldest friend, a Pakistani he knew from his Oxford days: 'My brother enemy. There will always be a place for you in my heart, but there is no longer a place for you in my country. The green and pleasant land is red with the blood of brave men, broken women and innocent children, and the calls for vengeance will not and should not be silenced. My brother, my enemy. It's time to stop fighting, and go home.'

Hassan

Kuala Lumpur General Hospital, Malaysia

Hari Hassan moves awkwardly in his hospital bed, and pulls out his intravenous drip by accident. The fluid splashes on the floor, and he looks at it with helpless irritation. They keep him on a drip because he doesn't drink enough water – he tries, but he can't. And so water seeps into him from one bag, and dribbles out of the tube inserted into his flaccid organ to another. The discomfort of the catheter is nothing compared to the unholy horror of moving his bowels; he feels envious of other patients with movements so loose that they can soil themselves in their sleep, and then get cleaned up like babies. Dying, like birth, is a messy, undignified business. 'You piss in a bag and lose your mind, /Forgetting the ones you left behind,' he thinks to himself. Doggerel verse comes to him so often now, he forgets what real verse is. He doesn't write down these snippets of rhyme, as writing has become a physically arduous business; the posture it requires, the need for fine, repetitive hand movements

12

which are now such a struggle for him to execute, the frustration as the pen scrapes and slides jaggedly on the paper; in his youth he had yearned to feel pain as he wrote, the anguished flame of genius as words were torn from his soul, and he had been disappointed that writing was so easy. Now he writes only from necessity; he writes letters to his son, or rather, the same letter, again and again, as his son has never yet responded; and the physical and mental distress of composing this letter, letting it burn in memory and rise like a phoenix, is a pain just as acute as the pain he had wished for when he was a young airman trying to craft his wartime experiences into luminous phrases, even more acute than that of his constipated bowels.

He lies to himself even in his doggerel – his writing has always been deceptive, not in a clever, academic way, it has just been taken for something other than it really was. It has occasionally even been insincere – when he wrote what he was expected to feel, rather than what he really did. He has lied just now because he hasn't lost his mind, much to his regret, as losing his mind would make everything easier and him much less accountable. He imagines his mind as a persistently yapping dog, real enough for someone to throw a stick for it to chase: 'Whose was that animal, which just ran out of here?' Nurse might ask disapprovingly, and he would answer, 'That old thing? That was just my mind. Don't bother chasing after it. It's happier out in the fresh air. I was hoping that some kind person might drive it into the forest, and lose it there. It wasn't much use to me anyway.' Although, of course, we never lose the things we want to lose, they linger and reek like dead bodies in the basement; Nurse will bring the mind-dog back, and chain it to his bed where it can't escape. And the mind-dog, knowing that Hassan wanted rid of him, will look at him with doleful, resentful eyes, and continue to yap persistently, torturing him now subtly and now obviously, for his treachery. No, his mind remains in muscular good form; while the rest of him declines, stiffens, shrinks and fades.

Cancer, he thinks wistfully, cancer could have been quick. Aids, if he had refused the drugs, might have eaten his irritable mind into confetti. Alzheimer's would have been gradual and provided absolution – he might have forgotten he had a son at all, and would have been freed from the guilt that this knowledge brought with it. A heart attack, so blissfully unexpected, a bolt of lightning, a benediction from the gods. A stroke, the first incapacitating, and then another, and then the final, deadly, stroke; if only he could whisper to Nurse to inject some air into his carotid artery, if only he had the means to make his murder worthwhile. All the ways he could have died, over the years, all the miracles that have kept him alive when worthier friends and rivals have passed on; he has survived a world war and Indian partition in the forties, years of civil unrest and then the civil war which led to Bangladeshi independence in the seventies. 'We're not dead yet,' he had boasted to his best friend, Anwar

Shah, some years ago, as though it were something to be proud of. If he had known what he would come to, he wouldn't have been so smug. He would have jumped on a train line or walked under a bus, while he still had the wit and wherewithal to do it. In less than a year since his first diagnosis, he has gone from hale to helpless. On his admission to the hospital, following the drastic worsening of his condition with the full paralysis of his legs and the weakening of the muscles of his chest, he had hopefully signed a Do Not Resuscitate form, hoping that his next choking fit would be enough to finish the job, hoping that he might die swiftly from respiratory failure rather than waiting vainly for pneumonia to reach him in his antiseptic cell, but his son had rescinded it, suggesting that Hari Hassan was depressed and not fit to make the decision. His son paid the hospital bills, keeping Hassan in the luxury of a private room, and the administration agreed with his decision. Hassan was worth more to them alive than dead. He realized that his son intended to keep him as his private prisoner, as long as he naturally could, to extend his suffering as long as was legally viable.

Hari Hassan's second lie was about forgetting; he hasn't forgotten the ones he left behind. They are with him more urgently than anyone he sees on a daily basis, the nurse who changes his catheter and his sheets, the spicy-sweet scented Tamil woman who brings him his food and now mashes it, on advice, to avoid further choking fits, the elderly cleaner who clanks the bucket of disinfectant around, and who has so far not left it close enough for him to drink. His thoughts are with those who are missing; the son who has abandoned him, who once lisped with comic timing when no more than three years old, 'Baba, you so funny, you so ridd-yik-ill-us!' with an inexpert mastery of those last four English syllables that had made his heart swell with pride. His son Ejaz, his little Ejazzy-Jazz, who has grown up to loathe his father and write pulp fiction bestsellers in Singapore. Of the daughter he himself abandoned, over fifty years ago; when Nazneen died – they said it was eclampsia, but he had wondered later if they had simply killed her in the conveniently bloody aftermath of the birth out of familial shame – he had let them take the baby girl away, to be adopted, they said. He wondered if she had been quietly disposed of too, smothered softly, or sold into slavery or prostitution, or whether she really had been adopted, and had lived a good and happy life, had children of her own, and looked forward to dying of natural causes herself in a few decades, surrounded by friends and family. His thoughts are with Nazneen, whom he knew for just a year, his first and only love, with her unaffected laugh and her cigarette and her tailored man's suit she wore as a costume; but he doesn't think of his nervous, worthy wife, who devoted herself to him for almost thirty years, whom he looked after but neglected to love, before her death in a suspicious do-mestic blaze. Perhaps he deserves to be here. Perhaps, in the end, all men get what they deserve.

He presses the button by his bed for Nurse, and after a few moments she enters. It is the practical Malay one in her forties, whom he prefers to the sympathetic Chinese one in her thirties. '*Selamat petang*,' she nods in greeting, and efficiently tapes back the drip. He likes the way that she doesn't look at him, she just looks through him instead, as though he already wasn't there. It gives him hope. '*Apa khabar?*' she says in her crisp way, asking how he is, while making a note on his chart.

He sighs, and replies as she expects, '*Khabar baik*,' although he is lying again, he is obviously anything but fine. He feels the urge to rebel, and annoy, and adds petulantly, '*Saya tidak suka bilik ini.*' Complaining about his room, as though he had some choice in the matter.

'So? You don't have to like the room,' responds Nurse in her native Bahasa, 'It's not a hotel. You're here whether you like it or not.'

Hassan absorbs this insightful comment; in a few words she has summed up his predicament, and that of every other unhappy being on the planet. He had never had that economy of phrase when he was a writer. He's here whether he likes it or not. 'Nurse,' he says, 'I'd like to write a letter.' Nurse rolls her eyes, but goes to his side, and props him up; he is as light and brittle as hollow wood, and she brings the tray to him, she presses a pen in his hand and places his hand above the paper. When she leaves, Hari Hassan scratches at the paper with intense discomfort; the letter, this same letter, changes in some details, but always ends the same way, with the

17

same plea calling across the state border to the centrally located Singapore apartment where his son Ejaz lives and works. 'Jazz,' he will write, again, and again until he is heard, 'we need to forgive each other. You need to forgive me. You need to let me go.'

Jazz

Little India, Singapore

Ejaz 'Jazz' Ahsan flexes his fingers, and then rattles away at his keyboard until he reaches the end of his chapter. He starts to read it back, and he is soon so bored by his own words that he starts to skim, and then skips to the end. It's not very good, it's not good at all in fact, but it'll do. It won't disappoint his avid readers, or his editor, or his overseas agent; it won't even disappoint his critics, who take lavish delight in ripping his work to shreds, in spite of, or possibly because of, his commercial success. He doesn't care about reviews, anyway; his father – who had once been described as Tagore's heir, with Wilfred Owen's sensitivity – had a lifetime of good reviews, which were pressed mustily into a manila folder like so many dried pressed flowers, losing their fragrance and ability to delight with time. He doesn't care that his work is dismissed as entertainment – he knows that people enjoy his books, he writes about men and women who fall in love and have adventures against backgrounds of international espionage and conspiracy. He provides escapist fantasy for those who need to escape, and sometimes, when he writes, he escapes a little himself.

'Not that I need to,' says Jazz out loud, aware that only he will be disappointed by this new book, and that his opinion doesn't matter in the slightest; he is just a small part in the publishing machine, just the bit which provides the words. 'Why would I need to escape?' He has a comfortable apartment a few minutes' stroll from some of the best Indian restaurants in Singapore, an enviable job, and a girlfriend who turns heads when she walks down the street. Home, job, partner – a tick in each box, isn't that how happiness is judged these days? He stretches out his arms, and checks his watch; it is six p.m., the end of his working day. 'Playtime,' he jokes feebly to himself, and gets a beer out of the fridge. He knows he should get washed; he is becoming a caricature of an isolated novelist, talking out loud to himself, failing to use deodorant, wearing the same clothes day after day; and tonight he is due to meet his girlfriend and a couple of her friends later for dinner. He tugs off his Chinatown T-shirt, printed with a large, possibly ironic, symbol for happiness, then his baggy, sporty shorts, and dressed only in his boxers, he goes to the bathroom, taking his beer with him. He turns the multi-function shower head onto the 'rain' setting, which reminds him of his childhood in Kuala Lumpur, running out with the other kids of his neighbourhood into their dusty yards at the first sign of a monsoon, with a bar of soap hopefully in hand.

He is about to step out of his boxers when he hears his phone beep. June, his girlfriend, is probably checking up on him; he goes to read the message with a little irritation, 'I'm doing it, I'm showering, OK,' he complains to his slim silver mobile. Picking it up, he sees a text from a foreign number he doesn't recognize. He flicks it open, and reads the brief message: 'Jazz, I'm coming home. Aruna.'

Jazz realizes that he has been standing there for almost a minute, barely breathing, staring at his phone. He dials the number and tries to speak calmly when she answers. 'Where are you, Rooney? I'll come and get you.'

'I'm in London, at the airport,' replies Aruna. 'So I guess I'll make my own way back.'

'London! What the hell are you doing in London?' cries out Jazz, feeling stupid for assuming that he could just drive out and fetch her home, like a knight on a white horse. 'How far did you think you had to run, for God's sake?'

'I just ended up here by accident. I married a guy who lived here, so I stayed,' she says matter-of-factly.

'Married! You got married, and you didn't even tell me. For fuck's sake, Rooney,' says Jazz in barely disguised fury. Something occurs to him, and his voice changes. 'You haven't had kids, have you? Is that why you got married, to have kids?'

'No, I haven't got kids,' replies Aruna wearily. Why is everyone so concerned about this question, about the full or empty state of her womb, even Jazz whom she hasn't seen for over two years? 'I don't know why you're so surprised, you must have started dating again.'

'Of course I did, eventually. You think I went to bed each night clutching a pillowcase of memories . . . sniffing your night cream . . . dreaming of your non-existent tits?'

'Still so poetic, I see,' interrupts Aruna. 'So, what's her name? And don't you want to know who I married?'

'It doesn't matter,' says Jazz. 'There's no point talking about her and him, it's not like they're you and me.'

'It's not what you think,' says Aruna. 'That's not why I'm coming back. I haven't changed my mind. It's just that . . . I wanted you to know. I guess we've got some unfinished business.'

'You're right, we damn well do,' replies Jazz. 'When are you getting in?'

'In about thirteen hours,' says Aruna.

'I'll meet you at Changi, at arrivals,' he says. He pauses and then asks, 'Why now? What made you decide to come back?'

'It was something in a book; the book you gave me actually, the collected works of that Bengali writer, there was something in a letter he wrote. I took it as a sign.' Aruna sighs. 'I guess that sounds stupid, maybe I've really gone nuts this time.'

'We're stupid people, Rooney,' says Jazz. 'I must be stupid too, because I haven't changed my mind either.' There is a long pause, as they both absorb sadly what they have just said; all this time, apart but not alone, and nothing has changed; a cause for mourning rather than celebration. He hangs up. Or perhaps she does first. Tears are running down his face, and he sinks to the floor, burying himself in the pillow of his arms.

Of course, he thinks to himself, this is what he has been trying to escape. All those books he has written, almost identical books, of ridiculously handsome heroes and mysteriously troubled women, who fight impossible odds and outrageous fortune, who escape death and smarmy villains and amoral Western agents and hook-nosed terrorists and end up together in a glorious setting, on a mountainside, by the sea, in the jungle or desert, in Florence or New York or Beijing, just so he could end their story happily, with a kiss. Just so he could escape himself, however briefly, to a world where happy ever after comes true. The cool, tiled floor raises goosebumps on his arms and shins, and he hears the shower raining in a soft patter; he catches snatches of conversation from his window, as hawkers ply goods and tourists seek restaurants and Little India comes to saffron-hued and cardamom-scented life. He can already imagine June's voice rising shrilly in anger, as she realizes that he has stood her up tonight. Over the border his mother's burnt remains are at peace in her grave, and in the same muddied-river city, his father's living remains are crying plaintively for the peace of his.

Jazz absorbs all this through the smooth marble of the floor; he feels more kindly disposed towards his old wretch of a father than he has for years, simply because his words have finally proved to have some worth beyond perpetuating his myth and his vanity; because his words have helped bring Aruna back. Perhaps it isn't quite true that nothing has changed, as at least he has been given another chance. A wave of calm suffuses him, a warm glow like a blush; he feels able at that moment to do anything: he will be a better person, he will write the best books he can with the small talent he has, he will be kind to strangers and kinder to friends, he will accept the weakness of others and the tragedies of the past, and he will, handsomely, heroically, forgive. The moment passes, and Jazz is aware that he is just a ridiculous, half-naked figure, lying on the floor, obsessing about someone who is walking back into his life as thoughtlessly as she left it. He gets in the shower, downs his beer under the warm drizzling water, and prepares to meet his girlfriend.

Aruna

Heathrow Airport, London

Aruna sits in a cafe at Heathrow, and waits for her flight to be announced. She has been lucky to get a seat so soon; the cost was astronomical, so she put it on their joint credit card. She will pay Patrick back as soon as she can. She finds she can't stop trembling, and when she told the airline assistant at the desk, 'No, just hand luggage please,' the woman gave her a long, searching look, and Aruna was embarrassed to see compassion under the woman's rock-hard foundation, sticky black lashes and plump, plummy lips.

'Are you all right, honey?' the woman asked, and Aruna shook her head instinctively, before she realized what she was doing, and nodded emphatically instead.

'Yes. I'm fine,' she lied unconvincingly, aware of how her hand was shaking as she took back her passport from the counter. She thought how good it would feel to have that woman put her round, matronly arms around her, and say that it was OK to cry. To hand her a clean, white

25

handkerchief and tell her to let it all out. Instead Aruna practically snatched her boarding pass, and stalked away.

She knows she shouldn't have taken Jazz's call; the phone call has given it all away; she has realized that he thought she was expecting him to rescue her, a damsel in unremitting distress, and is torn between being offended that he thinks her so weak and relieved that he still cares. Has he really been waiting for her, all this time, like some unfortunate prince in a fairy tale? She is not going back for him; the reason she left hasn't changed, the clean nature of her departure from London will not be sullied by the cheap hope of rapprochement, a return to an unavailable ex-lover. Jazz was more to her than that; her best friend since school, closer to her than family, her self-appointed protector, someone who accepted and absorbed the lingering madness she felt, someone who possessed her, in both meanings of the word.

Aruna's phone beeps while she listlessly drinks her coffee (more coffee! It won't help her trembling, and it'll make her even more clinically irritable than she already is, but she didn't know what else to order when the tackily dressed waitress bore down on her, and she assumed she had to order something so she could sit), and she glances at it quickly, wondering whether it is Jazz. Instead it is a text message from Patrick. 'Hospital manic. Have to stay for second shift – v sorry. Don't wait up. Love P xxxx.' Aruna looks at the message for a long time with acute bewilderment, as though as it is for someone else, and has been sent to her by mistake. She is

26

embarrassed by the generosity with which he always signs himself off, four kisses, as though he has grossly overestimated her worth. She has already left Patrick, she has left him for three whole hours, and it seems absurd that he doesn't yet know this. That he is working at the hospital, diagnosing and healing patients in curtain-partitioned wards, and is expecting his wife to be at home. She feels a coward for saying nothing, but now there is surely nothing that can be said; she can hardly call him at work and tell him that she's gone, or text him back telling him that he's the one who needn't wait up, ever again. But if she doesn't reply, she knows he'll call her, to check she's seen the message. After some hesitation, she sends a text back, 'Gone to see a friend, so won't be at the flat tonight. Aruna', which isn't quite a lie, but is just as cowardly.

Aruna has known Patrick for eighteen months, and been married to him for almost a year. When she left Singapore, she had ended up in London, visiting an old friend from university, toying with the idea of a research fellowship. She met Patrick at a lecture at SOAS, the School of Oriental and African Studies; she noticed him straight away, as he was looking with miserable disinterest at the opening exhibit, and not hiding his boredom at his date's detailed commentary. She guessed he was older than her, by four or five years, and he was so solid looking he seemed to be carved of wood; he was wearing a suit, a plain uniform which didn't really do him justice, but which seemed to be appropriate for the event, as most other attendees were dressed similarly. He brightened up perceptibly when he saw her looking his way, and glanced back with a smile. 'Think that big white bloke fancies you,' scoffed her date, a snobby Indian academic whom her friend had set her up with. During the lecture she found herself looking around for the big white bloke, for the close hazel curls that disappeared into down at his strong, pale neck. She was mortified when she finally saw him, as she caught his eye too obviously, like some sluttish vamp; he grinned conspiratorially at her, with a comedy yawn while eyeballing his watch, and a puff of laughter erupted from her before she knew it, which she quickly disguised as a cough.

There were drinks following the lecture, and after a few too many, Aruna excused herself from her date to go to the ladies. When she came back out into the corridor, she found herself walking straight into a suited chest; it was as hard as rock. She knew it was him before she even looked up, his heroic build not quite concealed beneath the determined ordinariness of off-the-rack tailoring. What did the British middle class feed their kids, she thought with the mistiness of mild intoxication, to create someone so tall and wide and hard? Under the conventional suit, he was like something from fantasy or myth; he might have been nurtured on Ent water, his parents should have been trees or boulders. 'God,

28

I'm sorry,' she sputtered. Her head barely reached his shoulder.

'No, I'm sorry. I should have stalked you with a bit more subtlety. At least given you enough space to leave the loo,' he said. His voice was as clear as glass, unclouded by artifice or insincerity; she liked his accent, the pan-British kind which betrayed no Home Counties horsiness, no gritty London edge, no regional musicality in tone. It was an Anywhere Accent. A fittable-in accent, the sort which might be developed by someone who had been moved around a lot as a child, an accent that worked everywhere. 'I'm Patrick,' he said. 'Dr Patrick Jones.'

'I'm Aruna. Dr Aruna Ahmed,' she replied, holding out her hand to shake his.

Patrick laughed, 'The trouble with these academic places is that everyone's a doctor. I lose my advantage.' He took her hand, but just held it, rather than shaking it, as though unaware of this most obvious custom.

'So you're a real doctor, I guess,' said Aruna.

Patrick nodded. 'I work at the Whittington Hospital, up in Archway.' He realized that he was still holding her hand, and let it go. 'So you're a fake doctor, then?' he asked lightly.

'Yes, that's it exactly. I'm a fake. It's like you know me already,' Aruna replied.

Patrick missed any darkness in what Aruna was saying; he continued to look at her with undisguised admiration, and Aruna, for a moment, looking back into his grave green-brown eyes, saw herself as he saw her, an attractive foreigner, a little mysterious, carelessly glamorous, with long, wild hair and carved pert lips. Her slim brownness, so typical in Singapore (where she was arguably a bit hippy, compared to some of the Chinese girls of her acquaintance), was exotic over here. If he was from Anywhere, she was quite clearly from Somewhere Else; if he fitted in, she stood out. She liked what she saw in his eyes; she thought perhaps she could be this person after all.

'Thank God,' he said eventually. 'I hate real doctors, we're all up our own arses and bitter because we don't have time for a personal life, because the hospital has to come first. There's always someone dying when I've got a date.'

Aruna couldn't stop herself laughing again. 'I see you don't believe in saving the best for last. Is that why you're reduced to stalking women in the corridor outside the cloakrooms?'

'Obviously,' said Patrick. 'See, now you know me already, too.' He looked over his shoulder with the first sign of anxiety he'd shown, 'Are you here on your own?'

'Sort of,' said Aruna, feeling a delicious, cruel freedom in denying the officious blind date.

'I'm sort of here on my own too,' said Patrick. 'Maybe we should escape before the sort-ofs catch up with us.' He said it as a joke, without any serious intent.

'Maybe we should,' agreed Aruna and, taking his arm, walked him smartly out of the building; he was too surprised to do anything but go along with her. It was no

30

longer summer, so it was fortunate that it was still warm, she thought, as if she'd had to collect her coat, she might never have had the nerve to do it.

'There's a great bar not far from here,' he said, regaining the initiative as they walked down the street. He glanced down towards her, then stopped and said, 'I'm sorry, I know I should wait until we say goodbye for this, but I can't,' and taking her suddenly in his arms, against the ornate railings, he kissed her impetuously. 'I think you must be the sexiest woman I've ever met.' He pulled back to see Aruna's dark eyes blazing like coals, her lithe body trembling just slightly; it was like holding a flame. 'OK, you can slap me now,' he said with resignation.

'What an invitation,' said Aruna, breathing slowly, trying to control the treacherous flapping of her heartbeat. 'Maybe later,' she finally suggested, and sliding her arms up around his neck, pulled him down so she could kiss him back, feeling the reckless, sexy, Somewhere Else stranger that Patrick saw in her, take her over. She felt tiny in his embrace, against his absurdly firm chest, she felt as safe as a songbird caught in the cage of his arms, safe in his delusion that she was someone else entirely. She slept with him that night in his flat in Bethnal Green, she moved in with him three months later, and married him three months after that at a riverside registry office. She tumbled into marriage in the way that leaves tumble from autumnal trees to the musty earth below, with just a breath of wind needed to persuade her to drift away from her flickering past, and settle on solid ground.

Hassan

Kuala Lumpur General Hospital, Malaysia

Hari Hassan has a visitor. He doesn't have the luxury of dying quietly alone, of hiding the shame of his decrepit, disintegrating body and his bag of piss; he is dying in a centrally located hospital in the city which has been his home for most of the last thirty years. Everyone knows who he is (a venerable man of letters) and everyone knows where he is (just a taxi ride away). He gets visits from journalists, from students, from academics researching PhDs, from historians; sometimes he even gets visited by old friends, but these visits are rarer, as most of them are dead.

'*Asalaam alaikum*, Chief,' says a cheerful voice. It is Khalid Shah, the son of his best friend, Anwar, who had passed away a couple of years before.

'How does a good Pakistani boy get such a good Bangla accent?' asks Hassan, pleased to see Khalid, a solid citizen in his late forties, with grown-up children of his own.

'It's easy, when he has the good fortune to get a good Bangla wife,' replies Khalid. 'So, how are you, Chief?'

'The usual,' replies Hassan. 'Dying. But not dead yet.' Khalid looks uncomfortable, and Hassan feels mean for being such a misery. He smiles to make it look like he was joking, although he suspects that his smile has the gleaming insincerity of a skeleton's. 'So, what brings you here?'

'We're selling our father's old house. Abbu kept some diaries, interesting stuff, he mentions you a lot in them. I thought you'd like to see them.'

'I'd like to, of course,' says Hassan. 'It's just that reading is so hard to do now. I can barely sit up . . .' he trails off, as he sees the disappointment in Khalid's face. He realizes that he is possibly the only person in the world who would be interested in Anwar's diaries, and yet here he is rejecting them in front of his son. He changes tack hurriedly. 'But I'll take them, if I may. Perhaps Nurse can read them to me, if I find it too difficult.'

'They're fascinating,' says Khalid, with so much keenness that Hassan wonders if he is planning early retirement. Why else would he care about an old man's musings, even, in fact especially, those of his father? 'I've wondered if they were worth publishing, but I'd like to hear what you have to say about that, Chief. You've been published everywhere.'

'Hardly,' murmurs Hassan faintly, appalled that he will actually have to offer an opinion on his old friend's personal notes.

'I'm still going through the diaries myself; but I brought the ones from the Second World War for you, and from the seventies. I loved the running joke you Indian Air Force guys had; it was like something out of Monty Python: "What have the British ever done for us?!"'

Hassan smiles, as the words pinch a response from his overactive memory. 'Forty thousand miles of railway. The glorious game of cricket. Lancashire cotton. The rule of law. Modern weaponry. Civil unrest. The opportunity to die defending Britain against the Hun . . .'

And Khalid joins Hassan in the final refrain. 'But apart from all that, what have the British ever done for us?' He laughs out loud. 'I've got to tell you, Chief, there's great stuff in those diaries. Pure gold.'

'Anwar always was the funny one,' agrees Hassan. He sighs, and leans frailly back against his pillows, and Khalid takes the hint.

'See you, Chief. I'll let you get your rest.' He puts his fleshy hand, rude with energetic good health, into Hassan's thin, veined palm, but holds himself back from shaking it with any vigour.

Anwar was someone, Hassan thinks, whose presence was more important than his absence. In his absence he left very little impression, and even Hassan, who had loved him, did not spontaneously visit him in memory now that he was gone. But leafing through his diaries, barely looking at the words, just seeing the familiar scrawl of writing, the affectionate overuse of punctuation, Hassan remembers. Anwar, the little friend of all the world, like Kipling's Kim, but his little friend especially; Anwar strutting like a peacock, barely taller than five foot five inches, with his meticulous grooming regime, and immaculately polished shoes. Anwar, always one step behind Hassan; one year behind him in college, published later than Hassan, with the help of Hassan's influence, but to mediocre reviews. Anwar joining the British-Indian military after Hassan, and ranked below him. Anwar the Punjabi, and later, as history and the British and the Nationalist movement carved up India, Anwar the Pakistani. Anwar with the pithy witticisms: 'What do the British call an illiterate Indian? A Wog. What do the British call an Indian with an Oxford degree? A Bloody Upstart Wog.' 'Ever since Tagore won the Nobel, you Bengali chaps think you're all poets. But anyone can be a poet in a flood.' 'Punjab cuisine versus British cuisine – the unbeatable versus the uneatable.'

Some thirty years into their friendship, they had briefly parted company during the civil war, when East Pakistan broke away from West Pakistan to form the state of Bangladesh, and for the first time the friends were on opposing sides, ideologically and politically. Anwar's military career in West Pakistan had been more successful than his various literary attempts, and he was a prominent figure during the war. But when it was over, he had followed Hassan's lead once more, and in the mid-seventies had left Pakistan, and migrated with his family to Malaysia. He said he couldn't stand the guilt, and Hassan, remembering the atrocities of the war, remembering how he had asked Anwar to use his influence to have the West Pakistani troops withdrawn, had never pressed him for more. Yes, Anwar had been the funny one, the lucky one – he had loved his wife, and was loved by his children – he had always looked up to Hassan, and he would have been surprised to know how much Hassan had envied him. He was the dead one now, too, and Hassan envied him even that.

'Saw your review in *The Times*, old chap,' said Anwar cheerfully, looking sinfully comfortable in his biscuit-coloured kameez and loose cotton trousers, as he strolled onto the shady veranda of Hassan's rented house. 'They're calling you India's Wilfred Owen.' Hassan was caught out reading the paper himself, a glass of fresh pomegranate juice by his side, wearing Western pyjamas and luxurious-looking slippers embossed with the Magdalen College crest. He was embarrassed that his friend had found him looking exactly like what he was – a dilettante with too much family money and English affectations, reading about himself in the paper.

'If only I'd died in the war like Owen, they'd have been calling me a genius,' he muttered, putting the paper down with a scowl, and raking his fingers through his hair, trying to look like a dissatisfied, tortured poet.

'There's some truth in that,' agreed Anwar, taking the cane chair next to Hassan's. 'But don't be so cross about a flattering review, you'll just end up looking insincere. "Bigotry tries to keep truth safe in its hand, With a grip that kills it." '

'That's rather good,' said Hassan, with unflattering surprise. Anwar didn't take offence.

'It's not one of mine, it's Sir Rabindranath Tagore's. The other great poet that reviewer compared you to; I was making a joke.'

'That's what I meant, old chap,' lied Hassan, 'when I said it was rather good.'

Anwar looked unconvinced, but then laughed. 'I sometimes wonder if you joined up just for this reason; to get the press behind you, to get the flattering comparisons. No one's going to rubbish the work of a war hero, even if he's some jumped-up wog from the Bengal.'

'You really think that?' asked Hassan, quietly enough to sound offended.

'Of course not,' said Anwar. 'I asked your girl for tea, I hope you don't mind, I decided to walk here instead of taking a rickshaw and got a mouthful of street dust for breakfast. My throat's as dry as the lamb chops you get at Mrs Sen's charitable luncheons.'

'Not at all,' said Hassan hospitably, raising his pomegranate juice. 'I'd join you but I'm already taken care of. So what were your noble reasons for joining up, then?'

'The same reasons as everyone, I suppose,' shrugged Anwar. 'It was a just war, the Japanese were a threat to India, the British promised Independence . . .' he trailed away. 'If I'm honest, I think I joined up because you did. I hated the thought of you being some hero flying up in the Indian skies with your hair coiffed like bloody Clark Gable in the movie posters, and me being left on the ground. I didn't want to get left behind.' Hassan gave an involuntary snort, which he suppressed quickly, but Anwar looked up crossly all the same. 'Are you laughing at me?'

'No, I'm flattered. But I think you're a bloody fool to think so much of what I do. Nothing I do matters – just look at me! I'm a fraud, writing about the horrors of war, and the massacres of our peoples, all from the comfort of my home. Inside these walls, it's like the war never happened.'

'What did I just say about being insincere?' said Anwar, picking up the paper that Hassan has discarded, and looking at the article again. 'There's no self-pity more nauseating than that of the wealthy complaining about their good fortune. Some people are just luckier than others, Chief. Time to accept it.' Chief. It was something that Anwar had started calling Hassan during the war, making a joke of his seniority; Hassan was unsure if there was a sharper nuance to this, or whether, like the casual 'old chap' monikers that they had adopted during their Oxford days, it was simply affection disguised as affectation.

38

The tea arrived, with freshly fried pastries. 'Wonderful, Ruby,' Anwar said to the maid in Bangla. 'It all looks delicious.' And she beamed, and fluttered back to the kitchen with a quick, light step.

'Stop charming the servants,' Hassan complained. 'They expect me to be as fulsomely grateful as you are all the time. And my God, what has she done to your tea? I don't think she'll ever learn to do it right.' The tea had been brewed strongly enough to stand the spoon upright, and with a generous addition of thick condensed milk, looked like a caramel, soupy syrup.

'I asked her to do it this way; it's a relief to go back to drinking tea the way I prefer, now that we don't have to be so British about everything any more.' He indicated his comfortable national dress to prove his point. 'It was all right in Oxford and London, but I always felt like a damn idiot wearing a suit and a collar stud in this climate. And I always thought that English tea was like water – only wetter and greyer,' said Anwar, sipping the cloying, strong-sweet tea soup with obvious delight.

'I suppose it meant something in the end,' mused Hassan. 'The Germans and the Japs surrendered, and we've got Independence next year or the one after.'

'We've got a gun to our heads,' contradicted Anwar, slapping flies away from the pastries with a loud smack to the table, as though for emphasis. He placed the net cover back over the food, to avoid any further aerial attacks. 'You weren't here in Calcutta during the riots. I was. Hindus and Muslims slaughtering each other, throats slit like animals. Children screaming for their mothers and getting crushed underfoot. It took days to collect the bodies, days. No wonder the British want out. And now the unrest: in every pocket of the country where there's a religious minority, they're moving out or getting lynched. We're not getting Independence next year, the British are simply escaping, and we're getting a broken state ruled by squabbling politicians.' He put his tea down soberly, for once no wicked glint of humour in his eyes, but, rather, concern. 'We shouldn't stay to get massacred by Hindu fanatics; or by Muslim fanatics who'll slaughter us for having Hindu friends. No one we know can help when a riot starts, it's like a fire that devours everyone, it doesn't listen to reason; when the bodies are on the ground, God picks out his own. The Mahatma himself isn't safe, and God help the presidents of the brave new republics because they won't survive the year before they get a bullet in the back. Partition's inevitable, Chief. And call me a coward, but I want to make it to thirty and father future generations. I'm going back to the Punjab.' He paused and said simply, 'You should come with me, Hari,' and he placed his hand on Hassan's forearm.

Hassan said nothing for a moment, touched by his friend's concern, by the gentle pressure of his hand, warm and dry from the teacup, by the unfamiliar sound of his real name on his friend's lips, instead of the joky, distant old chap and Chief. He looked across at Anwar's face, still so young and plump that a serious expression looked absurd on him; with a face like that he would always be the comic. He would never be a poet, for all his wit; he wasn't made for refracting suffering. If I had a brother, thought Hassan, I would not love him any more than this man. He shook his head. 'I'm not running away. I'm a Bengali, this is where I belong. This is the land I fought for.'

'And you call me the bloody fool,' said Anwar sadly. 'Promise me at least that you'll go to Dhaka, or Chittagong, if it comes to it. Stay in the Bengal if you must, but at least somewhere with a Muslim majority.'

'I promise,' lied Hassan. 'When are you going?'

'Next week, I'm travelling back with my cousin, Ali Bhutto. He's visiting at the moment, from Lahore. Will you join us for lunch today?'

'Not today,' said Hassan, 'I'm working. But another day.'

'Sure, Chief,' said Anwar, finishing his tea with a slurp. He munched appreciatively on a couple of the freshly fried pastries, some of his old carefree mood returning. 'Mmm. The scent, indelible. The texture, incredible. Result, oh-so-edible. I think you're staying just for young Ruby's cooking.'

'With her tea-unthinkable, result-undrinkable?' joked Hassan. 'Unlikely, my friend.'

Anwar brushed the crumbs from his fingers and made to leave, 'See you soon,' he said. But then he stopped and turned at the passageway leading off from the veranda towards the cool, dark stairs. 'You will write, won't you?' he asked.

'Of course,' said Hassan, deliberately misunderstanding his meaning, but not sure why. Perhaps he was embarrassed at the implied accusation that he might not, at the emotion he felt that in less than a week his best friend would be on the other side of the subcontinent. 'I write every day. I'm going to start writing as soon as you leave. It's what writers do.'

'I mean to me,' said Anwar. 'Not just yet, obviously. We'll be seeing each other for bridge tomorrow.' He looked like he was going to say something more, but then stopped himself. He lingered at the door for just a couple of heartbeats, and then said with a cheerful swagger, 'And I'm warning Bhutto that you cheat . . .' as he all but ran down the stairs.

Hassan thought about what Anwar had said for a moment. Of course, he did cheat. He had not seen much real action, real suffering in the war; he had flown above it, in every sense, and the deaths that he saw were clean and absolute. But he saw suffering in the streets every day, even though he did not experience it himself. That was the real reason to stay in Calcutta, despite the risk. *Dulce et decorum est, pro patria mori*, thought Hassan. Perhaps it would be good and sweet to die for one's country; it had to be better than watching other people die. He needed to feel some pain himself. To funnel a real suffering, the conflicts of people and religion and life and war, into shining verse, and become a real poet, instead of someone accused of copying others. Owen, Tagore. He was nothing like them; he had imitated them instead and been caught out in the comparison, like a ventriloquist with a puppet. He hadn't been lauded, but Anwar, his closest admirer, hadn't seen that. He had been exposed.

He called his maid for tea, proper tea, made the English way; he was less embarrassed by his Western habits if there was no one there to witness them, and began looking at his notes. As he was writing, he heard an echo of something Anwar had said, recomposing instinctively as he recalled it: 'The riot like a flame, devouring without reason. When the bodies are on the ground, God will choose his own.' It wasn't bad that; he decided that he should encourage Anwar in his writing, perhaps he had something of a poet in him after all.

Jazz

Orchard Road, Singapore

Jazz always feels vaguely out of place with June's friends; he is almost a decade older than them, and wonders if they see him as some musty old uncle. He dresses deliberately badly when he meets them, as he is afraid that if he dressed well it would be seen as trying too hard; he never attempts to follow fashions, in case he gets them wrong and ends up a figure of fun. What am I doing here? he thinks again, as he drinks more than his share of the pina colada pitcher to avoid making conversation; he has nothing in common with these women, with their crude sorority-house humour, with their artificial surfer-girl vocabulary, their inflated sense of unsubstantiated superiority. He suspects that he is with June simply because she is shallow and beautiful, and he is jaded enough to appreciate beautiful people, and beautiful things, for their surfaces alone; he's not absolutely sure why she is with him. June doesn't notice his distraction, her self-centredness is astounding, she never considers his opinion or attempts to second-guess him, and never asks irritating questions like 'What's going on?' or 'What are you thinking?' or even 'How was your day?' (And what would he do if she did? Would he bore her by telling her, or would he dismiss the interrogation with a breezy, 'Nothing.' 'Nothing.' 'Fine.') In fact, June is currently regaling her friends with some anecdote from her own working day at the ad agency, of which Jazz just about catches the end.

'And so, after all that, Tim finally finds me, and says, "Juniper," (he always calls me Juniper instead of June, he's such an ass-wipe, as though it's my fault my parents are like such total morons), "You'll have to mentor Reza, because Kapil says he won't do it." And I say, "Hold on, honey. I'm not mentoring anyone who's prettier than me, or skinnier than me," and Tim says, "You're in luck, Juniper, because Kapil wouldn't mentor her because she's apparently not pretty or skinny enough!" So I couldn't get out of it, and now I've got some total dog trainee dragging around the office after me.' June is Singapore Chinese, and now speaks both English and her native Mandarin with the same breathy American accent that she picked up from her west coast US schooling. She cackles with laughter at the end of her story.

'God, you're such a bitch,' says her friend, Hulan, admiringly. 'It's girls like you who make their brides-maids look such frickin' freaks.'

'Like, totally,' shrieks her other friend, Bibi. 'She'll make them wear mutton-leg sleeves and green taffeta ruffles . . .'

'And bows,' agrees June. 'Lots of big, kick-ass bows.' She pauses, and then kicks Jazz under the table, 'Hey, but we're not going to ask these two hotties, are we Jazz? They'll show me up instead of showing me off, just too damn pretty and skinny.'

'I'll say,' agrees Jazz vaguely, downing his remaining pina colada and pouring another.

'Wow, he's a keeper,' Hulan says to June. 'Most guys would run for the harbour if they heard their girlfriend planning their bridesmaids' dresses.'

'Christ, is that what you were doing?' asks Jazz in shock through his pineapple-mush stupor. Luckily the girls think he is joking, and laugh; he is grateful once more for June's natural vanity.

He makes it through another half an hour, until the girls start planning to go for dinner. 'Babe, do you mind if I run out on you?' he says apologetically to June, quietly so her friends can't hear. 'I think I've got some weird bug, I feel like I'm going to throw up, and I've got to pick up a friend from Changi first thing tomorrow.'

'No problem, honey-bunny,' says June, kissing him off dismissively on the lips. 'Call me tomorrow.' She always expects him to call, rather than the other way around. She shows no concern for his health – of course she's not stupid, he's obviously just drunk, not ill. She hasn't even asked who he is meeting. And she hasn't offered to come round later, even though Jazz wouldn't have minded, as he thinks that the release of inebriated, uninhibited sex might be exactly what he needs that night, a vaccination against whatever might happen the next morning, when Aruna gets off the plane. He feels discarded as casually as a mistress, and he wonders whether he might have got the dynamics of his relationship fundamentally wrong, whether he might be the trophy boyfriend, rather than be the one with the trophy girlfriend. He decides that he doesn't have too much pride to beg.

'Come round later, when you're done, if you want. I'd really like you to,' he says, looking straight at her, his hand gently resting on her thigh, so there is no way she can misintepret his meaning.

'Maybe I will,' says June, loudly enough to get her girl-friends' attention, and kisses him again, fulsomely this time, before pushing him away. 'But don't wait up.'

Jazz stumbles from the bar, sure that she will come. She likes showing her friends that she's in control, but he knows that she likes the validation of being wanted more. He knows he'll wake in the early hours to find her clothing him in her city-damp skin, gagging him with her silken hair while she sucks him in, possesses him, and rolls over to rock him in the cradle of her hips. For some reason, this realization doesn't turn him on, but makes him feel a little used, a little compromised, as though he wasn't the one who had wanted her first. Instead of going back to his flat in Little India, he heads towards the harbour, where the boats sway gently on the water, and the vaguely sweet, peanut-soaked scent of satay chicken and beef wafts over to him, making him feel that he really will throw up.

Jazz and Aruna used to sit and overlook the harbour when they were teenagers, and make out while the waves lapped on one side, and diners clattered cutlery on the other. He wasn't sure when they went from being class-mates and friends to being a couple. It happened so fluidly; they'd known each other so long, from before she had breasts, and before his voice broke. They were both ten years old when they met, at an English-speaking inter-national school. Aruna was born and bred Singaporean, her parents were both originally from the Bengal, but had lived on the island for years. Her first language was English, but her Mandarin was excellent, and the Bahasa she'd learned at school more than acceptable. Jazz was an outsider when he arrived from KL; Bahasa and Bengali were his first languages, and he still spoke his English with a Malaysian accent. But anyone coming into their class assumed that they were siblings; with their Bangla slightness of form, their fine lips, big brown eyes and long straight lashes. During that first year of school they were the same height, and people used to joke that if Aruna cut her hair and wore trousers, or Jazz grew his and wore a dress, they could be twins. Perhaps because they were expected to be, they grew inseparable; they adopted each other's family nicknames, Rooney and Jazz;

they adopted each other's interests, including but not limited to the works of Tolkien, Agatha Christie's detective novels, any science fiction, Manchester United, dinosaurs and the ancient world. As they grew older, adolescent and arguably more pretentious, they moved on to the works of the Romantic poets, Robert Ludlum's thrillers, the natural sciences, Malaysian League football, endangered rainforest species and contemporary art (Jazz favoured Lichtenstein and Warhol, Aruna favoured Dali and Miró, once claiming with painful teenage sincerity, that in Miró's 'Woman, Bird and Star' she was the bird, and he was the star). They shared schoolbooks and secrets, falling into step with each other when they walked. They were so generous with their hugs, and with their kisses, that Jazz honestly cannot remember when they first kissed properly, because it was as natural as holding her hand to help her off the bus, as natural as turning towards the light from a dark place. They were made for each other; their friends said it, they said it themselves, and believed it. Their identical eyes mirrored each other's, their mouths fitted perfectly. Made for each other.

'If we're made for each other, shouldn't it be better?' said Aruna, sitting on the sand beach at Sentosa Island, looking at the lights of the city twinkling across the water. They had finished their A levels the previous week, and had been celebrating with school friends at the water park. When their friends made plans to move on and eat, Jazz and Aruna had hurriedly disappeared together, throwing their clothes over their still damp swimwear.

'Shouldn't what be better?' asked Jazz, deliberately misunderstanding in the unlikely hope that she wouldn't pursue her line of thought.

Aruna gave him an impatient look. 'You know what. We've known each other forever, so there's no need to act so coy.'

Jazz shrugged. 'Maybe it's because of that, we know each other, we're best friends. So it just feels a little odd.'

'So it feels odd to you, does it?' asked Aruna sharply.

'I didn't say that,' said Jazz quickly.

'Yes, you did. That's exactly what you said,' contradicted Aruna. She sighed, her bare feet trailing in the white sand, and scratched the back of her tousled head thoughtfully. Jazz watched her short nails grating at the back of her recently cropped hair, a fashionable new cut that didn't really suit her; she saw him looking and stopped abruptly, probably realizing that it wasn't the sexiest gesture. Jazz felt a little sad that she no longer felt comfortable enough to behave carelessly around him, and a little hopeful that she actually cared how she appeared to him; perhaps she thought of him as a proper boyfriend after all. 'You know, it feels odd to me too,' Aruna mused. 'Maybe best friends just shouldn't start dating. How can you be lovers with someone you used to have farting competitions with?'

'It'll just take time,' said Jazz. 'It'll get better, it's like doing anything, we just need to practise. I mean, it's not awful, is it? It's not like it hurts you or anything.' He looked at her when she didn't reply, and nudged her with his shoulder. 'Does it?' he asked.

'Not really, not after the first time,' she said. 'What about you?'

'A little, when . . .' he hesitated under her watchful eyes, and bravely said it anyway, 'when you hold it. You've got a fierce grip.'

'Oh, bloody hell,' moaned Aruna, and put her head on his shoulder, 'I knew it. It's me, I'm crap in bed.'

Jazz put his arms around her, 'No, you're not. It's probably me. I haven't got a clue what I'm meant to be doing. I'm supposed to be making love to you, but it feels like I'm not doing any more than poking at you blindly with a home-made stick. I feel so stupid.'

'Is there anything you like about sleeping with me?' asked Aruna in a small voice.

'I like the kissing before, and the hugging after,' he said.

'Me too,' said Aruna. 'Maybe you're right, maybe we can just work on the rest. We just need time.' She didn't say what they were both thinking, that their time together was running out; at the end of the summer, they would both be going to college. Aruna was going to study at Durham, in the north of England, but Jazz, despite having made successful applications to overseas universities, had decided to stay in Singapore. His parents were moving back to KL, and his mother hadn't been well for years; he wanted to stay near to them. Aruna had been disappointed by Jazz's decision, and had openly speculated that Jazz might be a bit too attached to his mother. Jazz supposed that it was true that his mother had spoiled him; she had never worked, and devoted herself to him entirely. He knew that it was difficult for Aruna to understand the responsibility he felt for his mother, as she had almost no memories of her own mum; Aruna's mother had died when she was just three, due to unexpected complications in her second pregnancy. They had delivered the baby early, but it had died anyway. And then so had her mother. Or perhaps it was the other way around. Aruna had been left with a nanny when her mother went to hospital, and never saw her again, except in photos and a grainy home movie taken by a family friend. Her father, who had been somewhat older than her mother, and whom she had admired as a distant, authoritative figure, giving a formal kiss and cuddle on leaving or entering the house, sagely admiring her works of scribbled art with a distracted air, became more distant still. Aruna had admitted to Jazz that she spent most of her childhood wondering where her father was; she didn't mind that much, and when she was older, she supposed that he wondered where she was too. When he wasn't travelling on business, they shared breakfast, and often shared dinner, and that seemed enough for them. Jazz was her family, really. When she returned from university, in a few years' time, it was tacitly understood that they would make it formal. They just had to sort out their little problem of physical intimacy.

Jazz kissed her on the cheek, grateful to her for not saying any more about it. He had been worried for weeks, ever since they had started making love, that she might suggest they see other people when they go to college, that they remain Just Friends. And then he kissed her unthinkingly on the lips, and they started kissing again, properly, tongues exploring mouths, running over sharp teeth and soft gums. Jazz's hands were around her waist, and then gently slid up her back to her chopped-up hair, stroking her exposed neck tenderly. Aruna opened her eyes, and looked around, the beach was empty, and they were hidden from view. 'Do you want to?' she asked, and Jazz nodded, resting his forehead against hers for a moment, as though gathering strength for a thankless task. He smoothed his hand gently across one of her small breasts, and helped her slide her sarong up over her knees.

Ten minutes later, they were lying with their backs on the sand, straightening their clothes, exhausted at the tiresome effort of it all. 'Better?' asked Jazz. 'I thought that time was better.'

'Yeah, better,' said Aruna distractedly. 'But still, I don't know, just . . . odd.'

Aruna

Heathrow Airport, London

Aruna's flight is finally called, and she steps out of the garish departure lounge towards her gate. She is shaking so much now that people are staring at her again, and one woman, a middle-aged Englishwoman with a kind face and round glasses, even steps forward to support her. 'I'm fine,' snaps Aruna, swaying so much that she sits back down, and then as the woman moves away with a rejected, 'Well, really,' expression of disapproval, she calls after her, 'But thank you,' belatedly and a little plaintively. When did it start to matter to her what people thought of her? When did she start pleasing and thanking you and being variously and vociferously delighted and thrilled and grateful for services rendered, usually by someone whose job it was to do them, or someone who did it for themselves rather than her? Why does she now say excuse me when someone bumps her on the tube, or steps on her foot, or pushes her out of the way or shoulders ahead of her in a queue? She has clearly been in England too long;

if someone pushed her on the MRT in Singapore, she used to consider herself perfectly within her rights to push back, harder. There was none of the have-a-nice-day and so-glad-you-could-come and my-don't-you-look-lovely insincerity that gleamed in her English interactions. She is looking forward to someone pushing her in Singapore, just so she can push them back, stomp accidentally on their foot and maybe even swear a little in effusive Mandarin, just loudly enough to call down shame on their family and forefathers and future descendants. She won't say thank you any more, she decides, unless someone runs her over in their taxi – then she might, as she might finally have a proper reason, for a genuinely useful service, providing something she has so far failed to accomplish on her own.

Aruna is shaking, as she is an addict. Once she left Singapore, she embraced the accessibility of soft and then hard drugs, as she drifted through Thailand, and then landed up on her girlfriend's couch in London; in Singapore, where even chewing gum was contraband, drugs were unthinkable, impossible to get hold of, punishable by death. In London, she received whispered offers whenever she walked about at night, and found it easy to whisper back, and try a joint, a pill, a powder – simple, satisfying transactions, curiously clean in their nature; money changed hands, but the hands themselves never touched, and everything was zipped in sterile plastic bags. The drugs separated her from her mind, so she no longer felt the squirming madness, as though she had shut away the writhing worms of recent memory into a zip-locked plastic bag too; it was a relief, it passed the time.

She realized she had a problem, when she found herself on the street corner at night, waiting for the dealer, instead of him waiting for her. One such night, a drunk businessman, middle-aged, fat and Chinese, came up and propositioned her. She had smiled politely when he approached; because he was Chinese, he reminded her of home, and she supposed he was lost on the seedy, shady street, and just needed directions back to the well-lit main road, and the safe bustle of the tube. He murmured something to her, and she said, 'I'm sorry?' with unnecessary brightness, and an encouraging smile.

'How much is it?' he eventually managed to say out loud.

It was only then Aruna realized that he thought she was a prostitute; she could have laughed out loud, he had mistaken her skinny trousers and her designer vest as a slut's uniform. She'd come to London, behaved like a whore, and finally been taken for one.

'I'm sorry,' she said again, trying to sound crisp and offended. 'I think you've made a mistake. I'm just waiting for a friend.' She realized what it sounded like after she said it, like she was waiting for another client. And the truth was hardly better; if he saw the dealer turn up, she'd look like even more of a whore than she did already. Just another sad junkie turning tricks to get high, an immigrant statistic.

'I don't mind how much it is,' the drunken man said a bit desperately, the collar of his shirt cutting into the folds of his neck. The fat of his jowls looked soft and pliable, like rubber, as though he'd been poured into his stiff suit, and left to set. Aruna shook her head and looked away; he didn't leave, and just stood there, staring at her, his mouth hanging open and glistening with saliva, his eyes glassy behind his smeared spectacles, and so she started to walk off . He reached out, and held her by the arm, not violently, just enough to stop her. 'Please, look,' he said, handing her his wallet, pressing it into her hand so she had no choice but to take it or let it fall to the ground, 'You can have it all.' He took his hand from her, and said almost tearfully, his eyes not meeting hers with shame, 'I just don't want to be alone tonight.'

Aruna looked at him, drunk, pathetic, grossly un-appealing, and fought the urge to slap him in the face with his wallet. She also fought the urge to take him in her arms, and care for him cautiously, as one might an orphaned wild animal, lost in the woods, to bring him back to health, to help him find his lost dignity. She understood this poor lost soul, as she didn't want to be alone at night either. She pressed his wallet back into his hand, gently, and walked away, leaving him with his head hung, on the street corner. She went home, and called the one-night stand she'd had earlier in the week, the absurdly appealing doctor she'd slept with after tipsily snorting coke in the toilet of a worthy academic establishment. 'Can I see you?' she asked.

'You know you can,' Patrick said. 'I called you yesterday and asked to see you, and the day before that, and the day before that.' He paused. 'You didn't call back.'

She suspected that he was expecting an apology, that he wanted her to say please. 'So, I can see you then?' she asked again simply.

'Yes,' he said tiredly, as though he'd had a hard day at work. She took a cab to his flat, and began to make love to him as soon as he shut the door behind her.

Afterwards, she lay in his bed, waiting for his breathing to steady so she could dress and slip out of the flat without saying goodbye, as she had done before. She turned to look at him, and found that he was still wide awake, considering her. 'You should get some sleep,' she said briskly. 'Sleep-deprived doctors kill more people than faulty wiring.'

'You just made that up,' he replied, reaching to push back some of her hair from her face. 'I'm scared to fall asleep, in case you leave again. Like you did last time. You just upped and left without a word. Not even a note.'

'Why would I leave a note?' asked Aruna, 'It's not like I'm planning to kill myself. And what would it say? – "Thank you for doing me"?'

'I guess I'm just a romantic,' said Patrick, stretching his long, strong arms towards the ceiling. 'I know exactly what I'd write in a note to you.' Aruna looked at him sharply; the way he said it, it didn't seem romantic, it seemed a challenge. His whole physical presence seemed a challenge; the space he took up in a room, in the bed. He was like a mountain to climb. She hadn't realized that she was staring at him, glaring at him even, until Patrick laughed. 'My God, here I am thinking that I could drown in your eyes, and then you give me a look that can cut through marble.' Aruna turned away onto her stomach, annoyed, and found him undeterred, stroking the curve of her back. 'You know, I thought women like you were an urban myth.'

'What, you mean sluts like me?' said Aruna dismissively.

'No, I mean women not afraid of what they want, and who don't care what other people think of them,' he said. 'The way you just walked out of SOAS with me the other day; the way you came home with me. Like you'd never heard of the three-date rule. I've never been so turned on in my life. The way you left, even. And the way you came back tonight, no excuses, no apologies. I'm not saying I liked you leaving, but there's no neediness to you.'

Aruna stared fixedly at the headboard, at the dark whorls of knotted wood in the moonlight; it's the imperfections in wood which make it beautiful, she thought, wishing the same were true of people. In a moment of prescience, she realized that Patrick's misconception of her would last; that his first impression of her, as the woman in control, who needed nothing but knew exactly what she wanted, would be the impression he would keep, and however else she behaved in the future, he would always think that was her true self. And because she valued the misconception, because she was seduced by the picture he painted, of this astounding woman, who had none of Aruna's base and cloying needs, she didn't correct him. She didn't say, I walked out and went home with you because I was high and a bit drunk; I left without you knowing because I'd sobered up enough to be embarrassed that I'd behaved like a tramp. And I came back tonight, because I knew I wasn't going to get loaded, and just wanted to fuck someone decent until I didn't feel like me any more. His version of events was far prettier; he was right, he was a romantic.

Patrick was still stroking her back, up to her shoulders, and then back to the curve of her buttocks, his warm palm smoothing away the gooseflesh that appeared in contact with the coolness of the air in his flat. 'Speaking of eyes, do you know the colour of mine?'

'What?' said Aruna, surprised, and turned to face him, but he'd slid behind her, and started kissing her spine. The tingling that she felt was almost electric. 'I don't know. Green? Brown? Hazel?'

'Good guess,' he said. 'All of the above. But it was just a guess, wasn't it? You never look at me, really. When we're close, I mean. Even when we're so close there's nowhere else to look.'

'I think I'd like a drink,' said Aruna flatly, changing the subject.

'Sure,' said Patrick, getting up helpfully, rather too helpfully, at this ungracious command. His eagerness lacked pride. He must really like me, thought Aruna, or likes who he thinks I am. Wasn't it the same thing really? Perhaps, the real her could fall away without anyone noticing, like a tree falling unheard in the forest, and all that would be left was the unreal her that he believed her to be; perhaps it was only a matter of perception, after all. 'What would you like? Just a glass of water?'

'Sounds great. With some ice. And some vodka. And maybe hold the water.'

Patrick looked uncertain at this, but left anyway. He came back a few minutes later, with a vodka on the rocks for her, and the same for him. 'I wrote you that note,' he said, sliding it over to her.

She sat up, gulped half the vodka, and only then looked at his note. 'Please stay for breakfast. Love Patrick.' She glanced up at him, he was looking both nervous and proud at the gallantry of his gesture, 'Love?' she said, with half a smile. 'It's kind of creepy, isn't it, to say "Love" to a two-night stand?'

'I knew you'd laugh at me for that,' he said. 'I wrote it before I realized what I was doing.' He sipped his own drink gingerly, she could tell he didn't really want it. 'Besides it's just an expression,' he continued to argue. 'At the moment, anyway.' He lay back down. 'So what do you say? To breakfast.'

Aruna finished her vodka in a second gulp, and taking the ice out of her glass, she rubbed the handful of cubes down Patrick's broad chest, licking the damp, silver trail they left.

'Christ, Aruna, what are you doing? That's bloody cold,' he shuddered in exquisite discomfort.

'I'll warm you up,' she said, dismissing his complaint. 'And it's too early for us to be talking about breakfast. You don't think we're half finished here yet, do you?' She reached over and took his drink, and downed it too, before she turned back to him, sliding over him possessively, ebbing and flowing across his skin with the salty aggression of an inconstant sea. Like a mountain to climb, she thought again, almost resentfully, as she felt his hard, muscle-ridged flesh beneath hers; his solidity and consistency made her all too aware of her own shifting, drifting surfaces. Patrick caught her face in his hands, and stopped her just for a moment, holding her above him, staring at her eyes, and she felt that electric shock again, of pure physical longing. Of a lust that was so perfectly distilled, it was no longer Lust, but simply Need.

'Just as long as you look at me this time,' he said.

Aruna realized later, that she had shamelessly swapped one dark addiction for several others; the heady combination of drink, deception and unconditional desire. With Patrick, she would lose who she was and be someone else entirely, the person he saw with his mossy brown eyes. She would dash herself on him, again and again, like waves foaming against a cliff; she would be both the swimmer and the sea, and in her own marine depths she would try to drown the person she had been, and the reason she had left.

The next note Patrick wrote to her, some weeks after their first meeting, said, 'Stay for breakfast. And forever. Love Patrick. (Not just an expression.)' She had never intended to get emotionally involved, to need someone and become their need in turn. But just like that she was caught, in the false body of someone free-spirited and unconventional, someone who was admirable, who got what they wanted, who gave the convincing impression of needing nothing, and who was apparently far more lovable than her.

Aruna's shaking has finally calmed down. She is an addict, but she no longer takes hard street drugs; she self-medicates instead on drink, cannabis, cigarettes and sex. It was a quick, dishonest marriage, she thinks, but it'll be a quick, honest divorce. She goes to the closest Duty Free, and buys a bottle of vodka. Her coffee cup has been cleared away, and so she drinks it from the bottle, not caring who she outrages. 'What?' she says fiercely to a young blonde mother with a toddler, looking at her pityingly. She had smoked her last joint, which she kept in her handbag lining, recklessly outside the airport, as she obviously couldn't carry it through with her. She couldn't even smoke regular cigarettes on the flight. She will have to make do with vodka now, until she sees Jazz at Changi airport. Her first addiction. Her first Need. The one responsible for everything.

Hassan

Kuala Lumpur General Hospital, Malaysia

Kind-faced Chinese Nurse is on night duty and walks quietly into Hassan's room. She unobtrusively checks his pulse, his drip, his bag, and then puts an envelope on his side table. 'Nurse,' calls out Hassan weakly. 'What is that?'

'Go back to sleep,' she admonishes gently. 'It's just a letter. It came for you today, but got left in the office.'

'Where is it from?' he asks. 'Is it from Singapore?'

'From Bangladesh,' says Nurse, unembarrassed to admit that she has inspected the letter on the way up. She takes it as her due; her patients have no secrets from her; she takes care of their every private bodily function, washes them like infants and turns them to avoid sores. She wipes their arses, and their tears when they cry with the pity of what they have come to.

'I'd like to see it now,' he says insistently, and so Nurse switches on his light and hands it to him. She props him up at his request, warning that she won't be able to return for another half an hour.

Hassan scans the letter; it is from an old friend in Chittagong, as he expected. It is formally titled 'RE: Your enquiry'. The letter starts with some chatter about life during retirement and the state of the mango trees and the cost of his youngest daughter's second wedding to a 'hairy Frenchman', but gets to the point by the third paragraph. 'So the long and short of it is that after exhaustive communications with the appropriate authorities here in Chittagong, in Dhaka and Kolkata, there is simply no record of the birth of a baby girl to Ms Nazneen Ali, daughter of Mr Nazeer Ali and Mrs Muryam Ali. Nor is there any record of an adoption in the year you advised, or in any of the five subsequent years. I'm sure you already knew that births and adoptions weren't routinely recorded in the postwar years, unless requested of the administration – even I've had the devil of a time getting a birth certificate for my Roshan, and she was born in the seventies; she never needed one before, but now she needs it to register her marriage in France. The Chittagong administration told me that if you provide all the details, they would be able to issue you with a certificate of birth or adoption for the usual consideration, but I assume that your interest, unlike mine, is in information, not in simply gathering missing paperwork.'

Hassan sighs, and skims the letter to the end. He'd checked before, of course; he didn't know why he expected the answer to be any different this time. Hospitals might have been modernized, but records hadn't; he was surprised that any of the old handwritten ledgers had survived. Nazneen's family had their way; there is nothing to prove to the world that Nazneen Ali ever had an illegitimate baby, staining their good name and ruining her cousins' marriage prospects, nothing to say where that baby is now. Had they killed the infant, and buried her discreetly with Nazneen, in the quiet but respectable funeral at the family plot in Chittagong, to which Hassan had obviously not been invited? Such things had happened in India in the past: baby girls born to untouchable families in the villages would be suffocated gently by those who could not afford another mouth to feed; violated servant girls who fell pregnant were found drowned in the river or with their necks broken in the family home; unwanted or barren wives were found wrapped in nylon saris, soaked in cooking oil, and burning in their kitchens. Stillbirth, the midwife would say; Tragic Accident, the head of the household would say; Suicide, the policemen would record obligingly, before buying a gift for their own wives with their unexpected, slyly handed-over windfall. And even healthy young socialites, in private disgrace, died mysteriously in childbirth. It was possible, but he remembers the letter he received from Nazneen's aunt: 'The baby is beautiful and thrives with her ayah's milk. God is gracious, even in our grief. I will make all arrangements for her future care.' Surely, in the aftermath of the war, all life was precious; even that of an illegitimate girl. Why would Nazneen's aunt go through with the charade of the letter, and telling him about the adoption, if that was all it was? He sits upright in the early hours, bathing in the pool of harsh electric light, waiting for Nurse to return. He is ending his life untethered, the loose ends and unanswered questions floating in the water as carelessly as his discarded husk of a body is floating in his white sheets. And somewhere in this floating world, he hopes that Nazneen's daughter, a hale woman in her fifties with her mother's liquid eyes and reckless optimism, is living, and raising her face to the morning sun.

Hassan met Nazneen at the cricket in Calcutta, although he didn't know he'd met her at all. He walked in late, at the start of the second innings, and took his usual seat among his cronies from the club. 'Sorry, chaps,' he said. 'Was working. Don't know where the time went.' Fazel and Sadek clapped him on the back, but were distracted by the sharp crack of the bat connecting with the ball, and started cheering wildly. 'Who's up?' he asked.

'Khan's batting,' said a young man he'd not met before, dressed impeccably in a pale Western suit with a hat pulled down close over his eyes against the blazing sun. 'Working up to his half century,' he added in a disarmingly soft voice. As Khan hit another six, Hassan cheered too, carried along by the enthusiasm of the club. The young man didn't cheer, he noticed, but applauded, with soft hands that had the unmistakable look of money, which had never done a day's work in their life; he had superbly white teeth when he grinned. That's a boy, thought Hassan, who certainly didn't fight in the war.

Later in the clubhouse, Hassan was leaning against the bar, sipping lemon sherbet disconsolately, trying not to miss Anwar. He liked the other fellows at the club, but just not nearly as much; I'm someone, he thought, who can only have one friend at a time. His myopic affection for Anwar pushed everything else out. He had the same singular obsession with his work; because he wrote he did almost nothing else, even in a postwar Calcutta heaving with social engagements and dilettante activities. He had only come to the cricket because he had promised Anwar he'd keep him updated on the team's progress. He pulled a cigarette out of the thin silver box he kept in his jacket, and was patting his pockets for a light when a soft voice said, 'Allow me,' and lit it for him.

Hassan looked up, it was the handsome young man from the stands. 'Thanks . . .' he said, but then hesitated because he didn't know his name, and wasn't sure if he was meant to, '. . . old chap,' he finished weakly, feeling treacherous because that was Anwar's name, and didn't belong to anyone else.

'It's a pleasure,' said the young man. 'I'm an enormous admirer of your work, Mr Hassan. If I'm honest, I came here today hoping to meet you.'

'How kind,' muttered Hassan shortly. 'It's just Hassan,

by the way. I'm not even thirty yet, and Mr Hassan sounds like I'm your father.'

'I suspect that my own father wouldn't approve of me being so forward. Forgive me, I haven't even introduced myself, I'm Naz Ali.'

'So Nazeer Ali's your father, I guess,' hazarded Hassan.

'One of the Chittagong Alis,' confirmed the young man, 'There are several of us.'

'Are you named for him, then?' Hassan asked, taking a drag of his cigarette, wishing that he could think of some less tedious small talk.

'No, for my aunt, Nazneen,' said the young man, blowing expert smoke rings, and then apologizing with a grin. 'Sorry. It's a childish habit of mine.'

Hassan looked at the soft hands, the white teeth and realized how stupid he'd been. 'You've been having some fun at my expense, Miss Ali.'

'Forgive me,' she said again, and he wondered how he could have possibly thought that her velvet, husky voice, grated by cigarettes, could ever have been a boy's. She grinned, 'I couldn't resist.' She pulled off her hat and her daringly short hair fell like liquid to her jawline. 'But I really am a huge admirer of your work.'

'I'm sure I'll return the compliment at your next amateur performance of *Twelfth Night*,' said Hassan. 'You're playing Viola, aren't you?'

'This is my costume,' she admitted. 'It's so comfortable that I took it with me.'

'What does your father make of you striding around like a boy, on and off stage?' asked Hassan, wondering why he was sounding so disapproving, like some elderly betel-chewing *chacha*, when he really felt so admiring. He supposed he was still embarrassed about having been taken in.

Nazneen nodded towards her father in the corner of the room, and waved him over. 'He blames himself. He didn't have a son, and so he made me love cricket and crosswords and shooting. I've become such a suitable boy, my mother despairs she'll ever find me one. I think that everyone is resigned now to the fact that I'll grow old gracefully at home, reading the papers with my Baba like a couple of bachelors in our rocking chairs.'

Nazeer Ali, tall and quiet, walked across and joined his daughter at her side. 'Baba, you already know Mr Hari Hassan, I believe.'

'*Asalaam alaikum*, sir,' said Hassan, respectfully bowing, and shaking his hand.

'I didn't embarrass you today, did I, Baba?' asked Nazneen, squeezing her father's hand affectionately. 'Coming out in my stage clothes.' Mr Ali swatted away her hand with equal affection.

'At least you got a better seat, Jaan, than you would have done hidden away with the other women,' he replied in Bangla. He stood uncomfortably with them for a moment, and was grateful when an acquaintance came up to him and he could turn away. He glanced back at his daughter, clearly expecting her to follow.

Nazneen looked apologetically at Hassan. 'I just wanted to tell you, Mr Hassan, I mean Hassan, that I thought *Azure Skies* was a work of genius.' She reached out and shook his hand, a little mannishly. 'I'd be honoured if you'd come to the play this week. You could sign my copy of your book.' She followed her father and his friend, and glanced back over her shoulder just briefly. Her pale brown skin was unpowdered, and had a slight gleam; her lips were unmade up too, and her plumper lower lip was just slightly pinker than the other. She replaced her hat, and the cigarette in her hand trailed smoke behind her in a curling, wispy stream.

Hassan went to the play, later that week. Nazneen was undoubtedly the star of the piece, more beautiful in her boy's suit than Olivia in all her finery. Oddly, he preferred her in the suit, than dressed and made up like a girl for her opening scene; although his opinion wasn't shared by the other spectators. 'What a poppet!' declared an elderly Englishman, the leathery native type who had made his home in India, spoke fluent Hindi, and had no intention of ever leaving for the dubious joys of a damp terraced house in the Home Counties. 'Whose wife is she?' On Hassan's other side, one of the bejewelled middle-aged ladies, in a splendid silk sari, whispered to her friend, 'Twenty-five and still unmarried. A tragedy. A waste. They had arranged something once, but it fell through. The boy's family had lied about their land interests. The shame of it. Once a family has bad luck, it stays. And now look at her – these people from the provinces have no idea how a girl should behave.'

Hassan went backstage after the performance to offer the traditional congratulations; although Nazneen was considered unmarriageable, she was clearly popular in Calcutta society. Wearing the rose-coloured gown she had first appeared in on stage, her shoulders covered demurely in a shalwar, her blunt bob catching the light and her rouged lips laughing as she dragged on a cigarette, she seemed every inch the sparkling socialite. Hassan waited a moment, and saw that it would be impossible to fight his way through the crowd to Nazneen's dressing table. He felt surprisingly bereft; he had thought he was just being polite, and he realized now how much he wanted to speak to her. About the play, or about cricket, or the acclaimed collection that he had unimaginatively named *Azure Skies*, or Chittagong, or anything really. He caught her eye just as he was leaving, and she waved to him and mouthed, 'Sorry,' helplessly, indicating the hubbub around her and that she couldn't get through either.

Late that evening, Hassan was working on his veranda, in his pyjamas and crested slippers, when he heard a banging on the back door to the house. 'É Ruby,' he called, so the maid could answer it, but had no response. He shouted for Ruby again, and as she still didn't wake, started strolling to the door himself. He unbolted the door cautiously to the dusty street, and saw a young man in a pale suit, holding a slim volume of poetry in one hand, and a lit cigarette in the other to ward off the flies.

'Dear child,' he said, attempting to disguise the surprised pleasure he was feeling with a condescension that seemed unconvincing even to him, who was only a few years her senior, 'whatever are you doing here?'

'You never signed my book,' said Nazneen. 'Would you mind doing me the honour now?' There was no flirtation in her liquid eyes, but rather determination, as she held his gaze with a long, steady look; her eyes were swimmable, drown-innable. She was, he realized, the calm before the storm.

'Come in, old chap,' Hassan said to Nazneen, letting his avuncular pretence disappear into the air with the warmth of his breath. He felt that he had been waiting for her all his life, and she had finally arrived. He reached out, and held her by the tops of her arms, embracing a dear friend after a long absence. 'Come home.'

Nurse came back as she had promised, and she switched off the light, and laid him gently down. As she shut the door, she heard Hassan weeping gently in the shadows, 'Come home,' he was crying to himself. 'Come home, my darling, darling child. I've waited so long. Please come home.'

Jazz

Little India, Singapore

It is still dark as Jazz shifts carefully away from June, and goes to the bathroom. He doesn't want to wake her, and so he doesn't bother to shower, he simply splashes some water on his face, enough to wake him up, and shuffles back to the bedroom to dress, in last night's jeans, but with a clean T-shirt. As he shuts the wardrobe, he hears a slightly piggy snuffling coming from the bed; June is snoring. She doesn't believe that she snores, but she does, sometimes quite loudly. For some reason, this imperfection on her part suddenly awakens a tenderness in Jazz that he didn't feel even while they made love; June has her flaws, but she is here, she comes to his home, she comes to his arms and she sleeps in his bed. That simple consideration, that simple kindness on her part has to count for something. He bends over her, and kisses her gently on the forehead; her nose creases in her sleep, and she turns away from him, pressing her face against the pillows. He smiles and leaves the room.

On the way out of the flat, Jazz passes the low shelf with all his editions. He doesn't put them there from vanity, it's just filing; he keeps a copy of everything for reference. He hesitates, looking at a proof copy of his latest book; he takes it out, but then replaces it. He goes downstairs to his usual parking space, and gets into his car to drive to the airport.

Jazz has told many stories, as his shelf of novels testifies, and he knows that he has many stories yet to tell; but somehow, all these years, he has shied away from telling the real story. From revisiting it even for himself. The story of when it all went wrong. This is the story he thinks about now, although he is unsure whether he is preparing for his meeting with Aruna, or distracting himself from it. The hardest thing about telling the story, he thinks, or any story, but especially this one, is knowing where to begin.

Arguably it began with their parents, or even their grandparents back in the Bengal, determining who he and Aruna would be, passing down both old and new flaws, just like that British poet had said. The one who looked like a banker, but was really a librarian. Larkin, that was it; Larkin knew where the story began. But Jazz supposes that in the impossibly practical brave new world of story-telling, where stories are circulated by bound and branded volumes no less than 80,000 and no more than 120,000 words, he would start the story here, in Singapore. The Lion City that wears many masks: Chinese, Malay, British. State, Town, Island. The place where all his imaginary worlds coalesced, floating on the edge of the Straits that merged with the South China Sea. A place of unutterable beauty to him now, as the velvet darkness fades to white dawn over the freeway, and the neatly trimmed palm trees in pots line the road in serried military ranks. The place he and Aruna called home. The story would start here, and it would open with a bolt of lightning from above; a death on a stormy day.

It was one of the worst storms in recent years, with electricity that seemed to crack open the whole sky with an eerie, almost nuclear light. Power was lost in several parts of the city, and falling trees damaged homes and blocked the roads. Aruna's father died in the storm; he was in his sixties and he hadn't been in good health for some time; in contrast to the showy pyrotechnics about him, his death was as low key and understated as the rest of him had been. He departed life casually, with as little fuss as someone popping out of the house for a stroll; he ate his traditional Sunday dinner with his daughter, complained of chest pains, had a heart attack and died shortly afterwards. Aruna had been back in Singapore for several years when it happened, having returned ostensibly for post-grad work, but really for Jazz. They lived in separate apartments, to avoid difficult conversations with their Muslim families, but really lived together, and had resumed their physical relationship after college with rather more success than when they first started. Given Mr Ahmed's general frailty, his death shouldn't have been so surprising, but Aruna took it harder than either of them thought she would. 'He's dead,' she called to Jazz from the ward phone, her voice breaking into wild, guttural sobs. 'He's dead.' She sounded as if she was choking, and Jazz rushed to the hospital. He found Aruna stretched out in the chair next to her father, her forehead swollen and bruised.

'I gave her a sedative,' whispered a nurse. 'I thought it best. She was so upset she hit her head on the edge of his bed, I don't know if it was an accident or not.' The nurse took the still hand of Aruna's father, and showed Jazz the blue-black bruising of fingerprints. 'She did that in the ambulance on the way over here; she held his hand so tightly.' The nurse tutted sympathetically. 'They must have been very close.'

'He raised her by himself from when she was three years old,' said Jazz, uncomfortably aware that he was lying, as in truth a procession of servants had really raised Aruna, and she had raised herself. Her father had simply provided for her, and made an appearance at prescribed mealtimes. Their lives touched only slightly, glancing off each other; they hadn't been close at all. Jazz found out later that this was what really hurt Aruna; he hadn't been an awful father, but he hadn't been involved or concerned enough to be described as good, and Aruna suspected that she had followed his example, and not been a good daughter, and now it was too late to do anything about it. She had wasted the last parent she had left, and that night she went a little crazy with regret; the death had opened the floodgates for all the dark emotion she felt, for her resentment at being orphaned before she had a chance to have her questions answered, before she had even worked out what those questions were. On his deathbed she felt a stream of helpless demands rise in her, with no shape or consistency: 'Were you ever happy? Did you love Amma? Did your father love you? What do you regret most? What did you have left to do? What was your greatest fear? What did you dream at night? What sort of life did you want for me? What advice do you have for me? Answer me, damn it, you cold, old man. Answer me!' And of course the cold, old cadaver of Mr Ahmed said nothing; the only answers she heard were from mocking voices in her own head that twittered like birds, 'Too late, too late, too late, too late.' Aruna had silenced the voices by bludgeoning them from her forehead, with a sharp crack against the hard metal of the bed. She let herself sink psychotically into her grief, simply because she could; she was now accountable to no one, apart from Jazz.

'Miss Ahmed,' said the nurse softly, shaking her a little. 'Aruna, you've got family here now, to take care of you. You should go home and get some rest; we'll look after your father, and we can sort out the paperwork tomorrow.'

The nurse left, and Aruna, her eyes puffy and small,

her face a crumpled map of tears, looked accusingly at Jazz. 'Why did she call you family? Did you say that you were? Is that what you told her?'

'No,' said Jazz, wondering why she was fixating on this tiny point. He wanted to take her in his arms and comfort her, but she suddenly seemed too angry and distant.

'So why didn't you correct her? You're not my fucking family. The only family I ever had is lying dead in the bed,' she hissed.

'I was going to, but then I thought that perhaps she only let me in here because she thought I was a relative,' said Jazz, a little scared by her behaviour. Unsure what to do, he just stood there, and finally said, 'Come on, Rooney. Let's get you home.' He went to take her by the arm, but she shoved him away so violently that he almost fell back on the bed.

'Don't fucking touch me. Don't fucking touch me ever again,' she screamed hysterically. 'You're not my family, you never were. He was.' And she pointed accusingly at the peaceful, prone figure of her father.

'I'm not trying to replace him,' said Jazz, although he thought that over the years he already had. No wonder Aruna resented them both so much now. 'I'm just trying to be here for you. Like I always have. Like I always will.' He approached her cautiously, and took her in his arms. 'OK, Rooney,' he said soothingly, and hugged her, holding her tightly as she banged the table with her fist, and wailed like an injured animal. She made such a noise that the nurse came back in, and administered another sedative. It was several minutes before Aruna calmed down.

'I never told him I loved him,' she finally said to Jazz, her voice muffled against his chest.

'He knew you loved him, you didn't have to say it,' said Jazz reassuringly.

'He never told me he loved me either,' she said. 'I don't know if he did, really. But I would have liked him to say it.'

'Of course he loved you,' said Jazz. 'You made him very proud. When you got your doctorate, I don't think any dad could have been prouder. He said he always wanted a doctor in the family.'

'He didn't tell me that. He didn't tell me anything. And I never told him anything either. I never even told him that we were together; I was going to wait until we were engaged.'

'He knew we were friends; he probably knew more than you thought,' said Jazz. Aruna didn't answer, and he realized that she had slumped into his arms; he wasn't sure if she had passed out, or fallen asleep, like an exhausted child in the middle of a tantrum. He picked her up gently and carried her out.

She woke up or came to as he walked out of the air con of the hospital into the stickiness of the warm evening air, still heavy with humidity after the storm. 'Why does that keep happening?' she murmured. 'Why do people keep getting us wrong?'

Jazz guessed that she was talking about the nurse's mistaken assumption. 'It's just because we're both Bengali,' said Jazz. 'Just like those Westerners who used to think all Chinese people look the same. It doesn't mean anything.'

'But what if they're right? What if you are my family, after all?' murmured Aruna ambivalently. It was unclear whether she thought this was a good thing or not, and she passed out again.

Aruna's moods got worse over the following months, so much so that she was asked to take a leave of absence from her work as a lecturer in the Literature and Language Faculty. She reluctantly agreed to see a doctor, who referred her for tests, but advised her and Jazz that she was probably just going through the mourning process. The doctor even specified the precise stages of grieving: Denial, Anger, Bargaining, Depression; he explained that after these, she would reach the final stage, Acceptance. The doctor made it sound so easy, as though dealing with bereavement was no more complicated than dealing with an unexpected cold: Red Eyes, Runny Nose, Sneezing, Sore Throat. Neat little boxes that could be ticked off as she danced down her yellow-brick road to recovery. But it turned out that Aruna's depression couldn't be contained by a box of any size; it was physically invasive, growing with the vegetable speed of a jungle devouring human remains; it crushed her in a muscular embrace, collapsing walls to become the world around her. Aruna was completely incapacitated, the dark terror left her shuddering on the sofa or in bed for hours at a time; Jazz moved into her flat and looked after her. She was given tablets that helped, and eventually began to have good days as well as bad. On one of these good days she went relatively cheerfully to keep an appointment with the doctor. 'I think I'm getting better,' she said to him, 'I think I'm going to be OK.'

She and Jazz waited confidently for the doctor to make his smug, predictable pronouncement, for his I-told-you-so claim that she was finally reaching the promised land of Acceptance, just as he had predicted. Instead, the doctor smiled uncomfortably, said he had the results of her psychiatric profiling, and asked Aruna if she wanted Jazz to leave the room.

'Of course not,' she said, glancing at Jazz and squeezing his hand.

'We think you may have bipolar disorder. Manic depression. The onset of the disorder tends to peak in early adulthood, and sometimes it takes a stressful event for it to present sufficiently for diagnosis; it's not curable, but it's manageable. You've probably been managing it for years, somehow, without even realizing. And it may well be years before you have another episode like this. But if we're to prevent relapse, there's really no substitute for appropriate medication.' Aruna said nothing, but squeezed Jazz's hand so tightly that he later found blue-black fingerprints blooming on his skin, which faded to autumnal yellows over the next few days.

Yes, thinks Jazz, pulling up and parking in a bay at Changi airport. The storm is where the story starts. A bolt of lightning, and a death.

Aruna

Singapore Airlines – London to Singapore

Aruna drinks so much on the flight, on an almost empty stomach, that she vomits. And so she has to start drinking all over again, anaesthetizing her dry, burned mouth and heaving, hollow insides with the vodka, like medicine. She hasn't taken her real medication, the mood stabilizers prescribed for her psychiatric condition, for months; she hadn't had an episode since she'd been in London, and she'd decided that she didn't need the pills, and didn't like who she was on them; she felt herself smoothed into a featureless, fake surface, wood without the knots; the medication had bubble-wrapped her from the world, the sky seemed less blue, water seemed less wet, scents lost the power to evoke memory, and beauty lost the power to move her. If you take away my demons, you take away my angels too, she had thought; and decided the sacrifice was too much. I would rather die fighting on my feet than begging for mercy on my knees, she thought; I

84

would rather die awake than half-conscious; I would rather be dead than half-alive.

It is early morning at their destination, and although it is just late evening back in London, almost everyone is now sleeping or trying to sleep, trying to adjust. Aruna snorts with laughter to herself; as though adjusting is so easy it can be achieved by a nap. She wonders how Jazz has adjusted during the last two years they have been apart; outwardly, he seems to have done pretty well. His latest book was prominently displayed in the airport bookshops; he mentioned that he has someone in his life. Perhaps he will simply greet her with the nostalgia of an old friend, and require nothing more from her than an apology for leaving the way she did. At least he doesn't require an explanation, as he already knows why. It seems both miraculous and terrifying that she will see him in just a few hours; she wonders why she isn't combing her hair or at least brushing her teeth. She realizes that she doesn't care how she looks to him; she even wants to look unkempt and unappealing, as though her scruffy appearance will be enough to testify to her suffering. At least her suffering isn't fake, unlike the rest of her; it is like a weight, a parasite she carries around with her; like a pregnancy.

Aruna puts her hand on her concave, barren belly. It's telling that the first thing Jazz said about her marriage was accusing her of doing it just to breed. The reason they didn't get engaged and married as soon as she returned to Singapore was because they couldn't have children.

They were both pursuing their careers, he with his writing, and she with her doctorate, and they stopped using contraception, agreeing to get engaged, to go public to their families as lovers rather than friends, as soon as a pregnancy was achieved. She'd been ambivalent about the prospect of having a baby – she'd never had a mother so she had no idea how to be one, but he wanted children and saw no reason to wait. She supposed he also wanted something to bind them closer together, something irreversible and incontrovertible, and after their years apart at college, she couldn't blame him for that. But when no baby came she began to worry. Why couldn't they? It was as though all the disastrous sex they'd suffered through in the early months of their dating was for nothing, as though they still weren't doing it quite right. If she was honest, there remained something slightly odd for her when they made love, even though it was now enjoyable and she could climax easily; but she couldn't say that to the fertility consultant, that she suspected her body was rebelling against making a baby because she had an odd, niggling feeling inside. Some months after her father's death, just as she was getting over the worst of her depression, she finally missed a period, and passed a pregnancy test. That pregnancy lasted all of a few weeks, and then her body just evacuated the bundle of cells with slightly more menstrual bleeding than usual. The next pregnancy was longer, she miscarried at ten weeks, and was ill for days afterwards. After the third time, Jazz, concerned for her health, suggested they stop trying altogether for a while. And although she knew he was right, she couldn't help feeling betrayed by him, by his willingness to give up. She began obsessing about the reasons for their infertility, about the anarchic chromosomes that seemed so determined not to zip together, to go forth and multiply, about her wicked body that kept flushing out his unformed children. Perhaps, in hindsight, it was good fortune that she hadn't sustained a pregnancy, as they couldn't have stayed together anyway. It should have been a clear sign that they hadn't been made for each other after all. Who she had been made for, was as yet unclear.

A few months after their wedding, Aruna and Patrick had a Sunday lunch with Charlotte, her friend from college, and Charlotte's partner Giovanni, in a kitsch gastro pub a few minutes' stroll from the Bethnal Green flat, where the tables were littered with exotic beer bottles plugged with dripping candles, and the seats covered in shiny zebra and leopard print.

'I can't believe that this is the first time we've all managed to get together since your big day,' said Charlotte to Patrick, fiddling uncertainly with her eel pie and mash, which was surrounded with a luminous green streak of mushy peas. 'You and Aruna never seem to be free at the same time.'

'Sunday is about the only day we can ever do,' agreed

Patrick, spearing his own pie with obvious relish. 'I work all day during the week, and Aruna's always working in the evening, or out. Even when she's home, she's out,' he said, his tone halfway between being indulgent and annoyed.

Aruna frowned at the criticism. 'And God forbid that Patrick ever skip rugby on Saturdays,' she added.

'As though you wouldn't be the first to complain if I got unfit and flabby,' he replied, nudging her with his shoulder.

Giovanni, who had only tried a few mouthfuls of his pie, put down his fork and pushed it away. 'Patrick, mate, do you hate us or something? I mean, really hate us? Why the hell did you tell us to order this? It's possibly the most disgusting thing I've ever eaten. And I eat Charlie's cooking.'

'Oh shut up, Gio,' said Charlotte crossly, 'I think it's fine . . . or well, interesting, at least.'

'It's local,' protested Patrick, 'and traditional. Eel pie's a famous dish in this part of town, you can't get authentic ones anywhere else.'

'Yeah, welcome to the haute cuisine of the East End,' said Aruna. 'I told you to order the venison sausages like me.' She chewed on her sausages and parsnip chips with satisfaction.

'But you can get sausages anywhere,' started Patrick.

'The trouble with you, mate,' interrupts Giovanni, 'is that with this likeable and enthusiastic thing you've got going on, you can get anyone to do anything. Even order sea sewage in a pie with radioactive peas. You're just too persuasive.'

'He must be,' agreed Charlotte. 'He managed to persuade Aruna to go down the aisle. The woman with the coldest feet in east London.'

Patrick smiled, and put his hand over Aruna's, before pulling it across and kissing it affectionately. 'You know what,' he said, 'she didn't need that much persuading.' He said it with pride.

Aruna smiled back, just a little uncertainly; it was true that he was persuasive, or rather that she was easily persuaded by him. He had just needed to ask. Stay for Breakfast, Stay Forever, and then some weeks later, Marry Me. She had pointed out to him that they had only known each other for a few months, and that he knew nothing about her, and he had replied that he could no longer imagine a world without her, that he knew everything about her he needed to know when he held her in his arms, and that he was looking forward to a lifetime of finding out the rest. So she had said, 'Fine then,' or 'All right then,' or something similarly cautious, and had let his enthusiasm wash over her and make everything happen. All she had to take care of was buying her dress, picking out a bouquet and doing her hair. The only real wobble had been during the actual ceremony, when Aruna's voice starting literally wobbling as she said her vows. Just the usual watered-down civil ceremony vows, that didn't even mention love; when she got to 'to be your friend and care for you always,' she couldn't carry on, as she knew that before the state's representative and all the persons there present, she was making outrageous promises that she wasn't in a position to keep. Looking into Patrick's serious, pleasant face, looking back at her with an absurd hope and trust she didn't deserve, her voice broke down and she burst into tears. And Patrick, misunderstanding the reasons for her emotion, but knowing only his need to comfort her, pulled her into his arms and kissed her tenderly through her tears, holding her close until she calmed, so that people at the back who hadn't been paying attention thought the ceremony was over and started to cheer and clap. After the moment passed, the official moved straight onto Patrick's vows, which he said without taking his eyes from Aruna's, and held firm by his steady gaze, she found that she could make it through the ceremony after all, through their first married kiss, and then through confetti, through a wedding breakfast with champagne and salmon and a three-tiered cake, through a first dance to Andy Williams' 'You're Just Too Good To Be True (Can't Take My Eyes Off You)', chosen by Patrick, and finally through to their bridal suite at the riverside hotel, to which they disappeared in the middle of the party, prompting eyebrow-raising disapproval from Aruna's in-laws and nudging from their friends, and from which they didn't emerge for two days.

'It was so sweet when you cried during the ceremony,' said Charlotte to Aruna. 'So romantic and emotional. I almost cried myself, especially with the kiss.'

'I always thought it was a mad day to have picked,' commented Giovanni, who was washing away the pie taste with his Belgian beer, and shamelessly hoovering up the leftover parsnip chips on Aruna's plate. 'Early March. Guaranteed crappy weather. Was there a reason you didn't want to hang on for the spring?'

'We picked that day because it was our six-month anniversary,' explained Patrick, glancing complicitly at Aruna.

'From your first date?' asked Giovanni.

'Sort of,' said Patrick. 'We were both at this bloody awful lecture in town, and you won't believe it, but our eyes really did meet across a crowded room. Like something from a fairy tale. I think I knew right then that she'd be the one . . .'

'It wasn't really a date,' interrupted Aruna, before explaining practically, 'we didn't have dinner or anything. Or even drinks. It was more like first shag than first date.'

'From fairy tale to hard-core porn,' laughed Charlotte. 'I'd let Patrick tell the story of how you met to your kids,' she added to Aruna. 'He makes it sound a lot more romantic.'

'I'm not going to have any kids, Charlie, so it's hardly an issue,' said Aruna, sipping her own beer, as she picked up the menu to look at the desserts. Patrick gave her a surprised look, which she noticed but pretended not to. Her friends clearly saw it too, as an awkward silence hung briefly over the table.

'So, what puddings are good here?' asked Charlotte brightly, obviously changing the subject, and the conversation moved on.

'So why don't you want children, anyway?' asked Patrick the following Saturday, still in his mud-spattered rugby kit, picking up her morning's leavings: cereal bowl, coffee cup, juice glass, teacup and a plate littered with burnt edges of toast and smears of thick-cut marmalade. She didn't reply, frowning at her laptop as she typed up notes from a book she was reading. He clattered the crockery into the dishwasher with enough noise to get her attention.

'I said leave those, I'll do them later,' she said, and carried on working.

'It is later, it's four in the bloody afternoon,' he said.

Aruna looked up, faintly amused. 'Don't be such a nag. You always come back from playing rugby tanked up and spoiling for a fight. It must be all the testosterone-fuelled high-fiving and head-butting you do.'

Patrick looked at her in disbelief, 'Did you just accuse me of coming home tanked up? I'm not the one who thinks that ten a.m. is an appropriate time to start pouring whisky into coffee, and vodka into orange juice.'

'I said don't be such a nag. I'm still drinking on Singapore time, anyway, they're eight hours ahead,' she said with infuriating illogic. 'I'm going outside to smoke.'

'Sometimes you act like you're just on some sort of extended holiday over here,' muttered Patrick, following her. 'Like getting married and getting a job and having a home don't mean anything to you at all. It's as though you've got no intention of settling down; every time I introduce you to a colleague, I feel I should say, "This is my wife, but she's just passing through . . ."' He sat with her on the steps that led to their small patch of garden, as she lit up.

'Not everyone's as keen as you are on settling down,' commented Aruna. Sometimes he seemed so settled, so secure, that he was practically rooted to the spot. She supposed that it was his way of rebelling against his unstable childhood, during which his entire family had been dragged around the country and even abroad to Europe in pursuit of his father's career. Patrick had bought the Bethnal Green flat in his twenties as soon as he was financially able, tying himself to a mortgage in a then unfashionable but affordable part of London, while his contemporaries were still sharing rented flats in Fulham and Clapham. He had worked doggedly through punishing hours to complete his medical training, while his friends dallied with more lucrative but less worthy careers in banking and media. And he had settled on her with such speed and determination that she was unsure whether or not it was flattering; he had made the decision knowing so little about her, it was possible that settling down might have been more important to him, than who he actually did it with. She glanced at him a bit cynically; he was exactly what he had always intended to be, solvent, respectable, conventional; a home-owner, a doctor, a husband. And she was now a home-owning doctor's wife; his stability should have been catching – she couldn't decide whether she was relieved or disappointed that, beyond appearance, it really wasn't the case.

Patrick watched her smoke, and after a moment took the cigarette from her, and tried an experimental drag. 'God, that's disgusting,' he said, flinging it down and crushing it underfoot. 'How could you put something so horrible in your body?'

'I've had more horrible things than that happen to my body,' said Aruna, thinking of her miscarriages. Patrick, of course, didn't know, and wondered if she was talking about something to do with sex.

'And you'll need to cut down altogether if we decide we're going to have a baby,' he added.

'Oh Christ, here we go again,' said Aruna, putting her hands over her ears, and burying her face on her knees. 'Just shut up, Patrick, you're being boring.'

'So why? Tell me why you don't want one. What married woman in her thirties doesn't want a baby?' he insisted.

'Do you remember, when we met, you liked me because you said that I was different, because I knew what I wanted?' said Aruna

'What's your point?' said Patrick impatiently, clearly tired of her continual evasion of his question.

'The point is that I've not changed. It's just that the

thing you liked about me then, you can't stand about me now,' she said.

'I never said I couldn't stand you. I love you, you know that. I love you so much I married you and want to have children with you some day. I just don't get why you don't,' he said.

'I never said I didn't want children,' said Aruna. 'I wanted children once, I just don't want them now.' She got up to go back in the house, brushing the dust from her trousers. 'I didn't realize that it was part of the deal when we got married. We never even mentioned kids before last week, but now you're beginning to behave like it's the whole reason you married me in the first place.'

'Why did you marry me, then?' asked Patrick, a bit peevishly.

'Because you asked me,' she replied simply, and went back to the garden door that led through to their lounge. She stood there for a moment, and then asked straightforwardly, 'So are you going to stay there sulking, or come in?'

Sighing, Patrick got up, and followed her back into the flat. He went through to the bathroom, stripping off his muddy kit, and stepped into the shower. He was under the water when Aruna opened the bathroom door, letting in a draft that fluttered the curtain. She knew she owed him some sort of explanation, but instead just found herself making excuses. 'I couldn't be a mother right now. You know I couldn't. I've got so many things taking up space in my head, I'm just so self-obsessed. I couldn't do it.'

'You shouldn't make everything into such hard work,' said Patrick as he turned towards her; she could see the warm rush of hope in his face, that she hadn't yet closed off the whole discussion, that she cared enough to keep talking. He soaped himself with efficient circles working down his torso, and shook the water from his hair. 'You over-think everything. You should just stop and relax and enjoy the moment, sometimes. Any moment. And frankly if a teenager who gets pregnant after a few too many tequila slammers in a club can be a mother, so can you.'

Aruna looked at him with some admiration, he always knew what he wanted, at least, and was never afraid to ask for it. He wasn't even afraid of asking the big, scary questions, when he had no guarantee what the answer would be. Stay for Breakfast. Stay Forever. Marry Me. Have My Child. 'I meant it when I said you're always a bit more argumentative when you come back from rugby,' she said. 'Do you learned amateurs sit around a bottle of chardonnay afterwards like a load of house-wives and complain about your marriages?'

'Most of the guys complain that they're not getting laid enough, that their wives or girlfriends are too tired, too busy, too stressed, too whatever,' he shrugged. 'They look at me suspiciously when I don't join in the chorus.'

'You don't talk about personal things, then,' asked Aruna, slightly relieved.

'Sure I do. Just not sexual things; they'd only be

jealous, and I don't want them leching after you any more than they do already, imagining you on the kitchen table or the upstairs landing every time they see us at a work function.'

The kitchen table, the upstairs landing, the sofa, the armchair, the bath, against the wall, on the floor, on the garden bench, on the muddy lawn in the rain, in the park, in the cinema, in the restaurant, in the car, in a cab, in her shared faculty office, in a supplies closet at the hospital. Almost every time instigated by Aruna – she was amazed he couldn't see that she had a problem. 'What sort of personal things?' asked Aruna warily.

'Well, when I mentioned that you said you didn't want to have a baby, Michael said that I should just knock you up when I was ready for one. Snip a condom or switch your pills, jab you in your sleep with a hormone to time your ovulation, shag you twelve hours later.'

'How sweet,' said Aruna. 'Now there's a healthy way to create the miracle of life. Deceive, cheat and secretly drug your loved ones. You blokes have all the answers, don't you?'

'Christ, Aruna,' said Patrick, rinsing himself off. 'You're the one who's like the bloke in this relationship; you drink too much, smoke too much, and leave the place a mess . . .' He paused, but only to turn and rinse his back. 'And you live on the sofa, you don't want kids and you always want sex when I'm knackered.'

'Well, at least I do still fuck you,' she said matter-of-factly. 'How knackered are you now?'

Patrick looked at her, and started laughing. 'Come here,' he said. She didn't move, but stayed exactly where she was, leaning against the doorframe with that half-smile playing around her lips, and so he got out of the shower, picked her up, and carried her back in with him under the water. He peeled off her soaking top, and began to kiss her passionately. 'It wouldn't kill you to let me in occasionally,' he said, 'in here,' and brushed her temples gently with his thumbs. 'I hate all our bickering.' She slid off her trousers and underwear, and let him lift her up against the dripping tiled wall, so she could wrap her legs around him, binding herself to him like a weed, like a parasitic ivy, and take her agonizingly necessary fix of him. 'Look at me, remember,' said Patrick. And so Aruna did, her arms around his heroically solid neck, and she stared into his eyes, the colour of leaves and earth, and could imagine for a moment, quite clearly, the forests his ancestors might have come from. But it was just for a moment, as the intimacy was too much and she was forced to look away – she thought he saw too much when he looked back.

'Sometimes I think you just married me for the sex,' murmured Patrick, his mouth close to her ear, only half-joking. Sometimes Aruna thought he might be right. She craved sex addictively, but used it evasively, as a means to avoid intimacy. She was happy to let him inside her, just not inside her womb, or inside her head. She was too scared of the bodies and ghosts he might find there.

Hassan

Kuala Lumpur General Hospital, Malaysia

At first light, Hari Hassan is surprised to see kind-faced Chinese Nurse return, even though her shift should have ended, and that she has not returned alone. He recognizes the man she has brought as one of the senior doctors, even though he has not yet put on his white jacket, and looks dressed for the golf course rather than the hospital. '*Selamat pagi*,' he says politely. 'Two visitors out of hours – to what do I owe the pleasure?'

'Nurse Xiang was worried about you,' says Golf Doctor. 'She says that you're not sleeping well, that you appear to be having nightmares, and calling out.'

'I don't remember having any nightmares and calling out,' says Hassan bluntly, casting an aggrieved look at kind-faced Nurse. It is bad enough that his body, right down to his privates, is no longer private; veins and bladder and gut open to whatever they want to pour in or extract from him. Now even his memories and secret sorrows aren't his own.

'It was probably night terrors, then,' says Golf Doctor briskly. 'If you really don't remember them. Rare for someone your age, in absence of a trauma or abuse. Could be the medication you're on, so we'll review it. And I think it might be a good idea if you saw Dr Rahman, just to talk things through.'

'You mean the consultant psychiatrist?' says Hassan in disbelief. 'What on earth do I have to say to her?'

'Sometimes just talking it through makes things easier,' says Golf Doctor with annoying triteness. Hassan resists the urge to tell him that for advice like that, he'd have to go all the way to the problem page of a teen magazine. 'Nurse Xiang tells me that you've developed some obsessive tendencies.' He pats Hassan's dead leg in an over-familiar manner, 'You could be with us for some time yet, before the disease takes its course. You want to be comfortable, don't you? We all need "Peace of Mind".'

He says 'Peace of Mind' in English, and the phrase seems ridiculous in the context of the Bahasa they had been speaking. With the same incongruity as one might say an international brand name in conversation, like Sunsilk or Shell. As though Peace of Mind was just another foreign import that Malaysia was selling, and the doctor was following hospital policy in promoting.

'Oh just piss off,' says Hassan, taking it as his dying right to play the offensive, belligerent old man. Golf Doctor shakes his head, and makes a note on the chart, probably something like, 'Inappropriate behaviour and response, sign of mental disturbance?' and leaves the room with Nurse. 'Dr Rahman will come and see you when she can, today.' Of course, thinks Hassan tiredly, they don't even need to make an appointment with me. I'm always here, aren't I? He has nothing private; he has no place to escape. He sinks back into his bed, where it feels as though his body is gently receding, making a slightly smaller imprint each day; he hopes that soon he might wake up to find that he is quite transparent, and his body is nothing more than a trail of dust on the bed that can be easily swept away.

'I'm so sorry,' said Hassan to Nazneen, as she sat beside him in the walled privacy of his garden, swinging on the seat just gently. 'We should have been more careful.'

'I'm not sorry,' said Nazneen, putting her hand over his. 'I'm ecstatic. It's the best news in the world. A baby, a blessing. You should be pleased.'

'Of course I'm pleased,' lied Hassan, 'but don't be naive, old chap. I've put you in an impossible situation. You may think that your family's liberal, but they're not going to take this well.' He paused. 'We'll get married, obviously. As soon as we can.'

'Now who's being naive?' teased Nazneen. 'First of all, you haven't asked me. Second of all, I haven't accepted. And third of all, I don't think my Baba will let you near me now, let alone take you in as a son-in-law.'

'So what will we do?' asked Hassan.

'What will I do, you mean? I'll talk to my family. They love me. We'll work something out.' Hassan wasn't convinced about the wisdom of this; Nazneen made everything seem so breezy, as uncomplicated as her life had been up until now, the adored only child of a wealthy family, who let her run free and do whatever she wanted. She might have been unconventional before, in her hair and dress and manner, but she had always been respectable. Every family had limits, had a point where they bent so much that they would break, and he was sure that this was it.

'We could just run away, you know. Elope,' he said, trying not to sound too off-puttingly desperate. 'We could go to Anwar's place in Lahore, and then on to Europe.' He saw Nazneen look at him with amusement at his discomfort, and so tried to make the proposition sound courageous rather than cowardly. 'It would be an adventure.'

'Lahore's too dry, and Europe's too wet,' said Nazneen dismissively. 'And don't you think that a baby is adventure enough?' She squeezed his hand, and smoothing away his frown, kissed him reassuringly. 'There's really no need to be so dramatic; let me talk to them first.'

Later, Hassan cursed himself for being so easily swayed by Nazneen's ridiculous optimism and calmness, for not taking her in his arms, on a plane and far away from anyone who could keep them apart. That evening he received a visit from Nazeer Ali.

'You'll have some tea, sir?' he offered politely to Nazneen's glowering, palely-furious father, trying to remain outwardly calm, so they could get down to negotiating the serious business of his future with Nazneen.

Nazeer Ali walked up close to Hassan, his face inches from his, and spat at him. He then took out a gleaming pistol from his jacket, and held it against Hassan's neck, where the metal felt surprisingly cool, like a caress, before the barrel was pressed deep into his flesh. 'If I were in Chittagong, you *kuttar bacha shorer bacha*, you bastard son of dogs and pigs, I would blow out your brains and have your sorry body dragged out to the forest to get eaten by your own kind. And I would tell my good friend the Chief of Police that you had a hunting accident,' said Mr Ali quietly. Hassan realized that he had mistaken Mr Ali's quietness for timidity, and that his calm, apparently diffident manner concealed a far greater menace than anyone might have expected.

'Sir, please let me explain . . .' Hassan began, but was stopped as Mr Ali whipped the gun suddenly and viciously against his throat, silencing him.

'And you deserve nothing better – you have destroyed my daughter. She will never marry now, never give me grandchildren. She'll live her life as an outcast with a bastard child.'

'I want to marry her,' Hassan whispered with discomfort, his throat bruised, the gun still held awkwardly against him. 'You'll have a grandchild soon.' He tried to remember the words that Nazneen had used, which had seemed so rich in hope and happiness, and repeated them. 'A blessing,' he finally choked out.

Mr Ali struck him on the head with the gun; Hassan fell to the floor, blood flowing freely from his temple. 'You are not suitable,' Mr Ali said with chilling poise, kicking him in the face viciously. He sat down on a cane chair and nudged Hassan away with his foot. Hassan carefully got up, and sat on the other chair, not taking his eyes off Mr Ali. 'Of course, I blame myself. I loved her like a son, and gave her all the liberty of one. So she wanted to watch cricket like a man, instead of cowering in the shade like a woman. So she wanted to do a little play, now and again. So she wanted to cultivate a poet who flew planes for the British and licked Churchill's arse. So she began meeting with this man who betrays his own Muslim brothers, freely associating with Hindus and Sikhs, even after they have destroyed our people in the streets. So this, so that . . .' he trailed away. 'I blame myself, I gave her too much education, too much freedom, too much free will. She wants to keep the child. We could get rid of it now, and no one would ever know, and life would go on. But she wants to keep the child. And so we are ruined.'

Mr Ali got up to leave and looked with some satisfaction at Hassan's bloody face. 'The best I can do now is to keep her hidden until the baby comes, and persuade her to have it adopted. We will say that she is ill,

104

something infectious, no visitors.' As he reached the door to the veranda, he turned back. 'I love my daughter,' he said. 'I love her too much to have her live her life as an outcast. To have people whispering, 'Whore', behind her back. I am only doing what I need to do.'

'Where's Nazneen?' Hassan managed to choke out through the blood and swelling, terrified for her.

'Already on her way to Chittagong, with her mother and aunt.' Mr Ali raised the gun thoughtfully, pointed it at Hassan, and added, 'I wouldn't advise you visiting. It is not a safe area for those who don't know it well. Too many hunting accidents, *old sport.*' He said the last phrase in English, mimicking Hassan's own accent, with a slight smile. He felt relaxed enough to mock him, clearly believing that his visit had achieved what he required. He nodded politely to Ruby, who had just arrived on the veranda with the tea, and left.

'Merciful Allah,' cried Ruby, seeing Hassan crumpled and bloody in the chair. The tea tray went clattering across the veranda floor, and she ran over to help him.

Hassan was terrified for Nazneen, and even more so when he received her letters, passed on by the aunt for whom she was named. She clearly had no idea of her father's visit to Hassan; she had no idea of what he was capable. She saw just what she had always seen, a quiet, considerate father, caring for his family.

'Of course it is a bore to be in Chittagong, and to be stuck in the house all day, but at least it is a big house, and there is plenty to do. I'm learning how to cook, can you believe, and to sew, all useful things for when our baby comes. Please don't think that Baba is being harsh; he is only insisting on this because he cares so much. I didn't realize before that it's not just my reputation we needed to think about, I have several cousins who are all getting to the age for marriage, and it would be terrible if we ruined their prospects. I'm so looking forward to when the baby comes. I know that Baba will change his mind about you then. He couldn't be lovelier to me, really. We sit together in the evenings and do the crosswords, and he says how much he'll miss me when I'm gone. I'm sure that when the baby comes, we'll be able to get married. Perhaps Lahore or Europe wouldn't be so bad. Perhaps we could have your adventure after all.'

The bald telegram announcing her death a few months later gave no details. Hassan collapsed into despair and self-loathing that he hadn't done anything to prevent it, that he hadn't stormed the Chittagong house and taken her away; he had told himself it would be better to go when she had the baby, but he realized that had been a cowardly justification, delaying the inevitable just because he was afraid. He knew that Mr Ali would kill him on sight in Chittagong, but that wasn't enough reason not to go; he should have saved Nazneen, he should have died trying. He learned nothing more about the circumstances of her death until he received the letter from her aunt. The baby had come early, the letter explained. And Nazneen had died shortly after the birth. A family doctor had attended; it was almost certainly eclampsia, and there was nothing that could have been done about it. She had found parents for the baby, a childless couple who were emigrating; the mother was already in love with Nazneen's little girl and visited her daily. The arrangements would be made. And Hassan, blindly in his grief and guilt, let her take care of it. He never saw their child, not even a photograph. He never knew her name. He still didn't know now if Nazneen really had died of natural causes, or whether she'd been murdered by her loving father.

'Mr Hassan,' says a crisp-looking woman in a beige suit, 'I'm Dr Rahman, I believe you were expecting me.'

Hassan looks at her wearily. He considers ignoring her, but finds he can't be that rude; probably because she is a woman. 'Dr Rahman, I'm afraid that the good doctor has wasted your time. I really have nothing to say to you,' he says politely.

Dr Rahman sits on the chair beside the bed, takes out a bound book, and makes a note. When it is clear that Hassan is going to say nothing more, she smiles and nods.

'It is difficult, I know, to speak about the things that trouble us. I understand that you feel I am intruding, but that is not my intention. I'm here to help.'

Hassan feels himself tremble with annoyance at the platitudes. 'You can do nothing to help,' he snaps. What does this woman, with her cheap pressed suit and her good shoes, who probably keeps a weekly date at Lim's Shiny Beauty hairdressing salon and has teenage children who eat too much junk food, this woman who works in a reputable hospital, complaining about tax hikes and the sexual content of imported movies and chilli-sauce stains on the soft furnishings and the termite nest in her garden, what does this woman with her ordinary cares think she can do for him? Can she wipe away the tragedies of the past with a magic wand, or solve a fifty-year-old crime, or find a child who disappeared as untraceably in the world as a tear in the rain? Can she make right what he had made wrong, provide absolution and wash his muddy soul? Even God, he thinks, can't change the past.

Dr Rahman makes another note, probably 'angry and uncommunicative' again, thinks Hassan, and then says pleasantly, 'You're right. If you do not wish to talk to me, I can do nothing to help. You have night terrors, Mr Hassan, you have been showing obsessive behaviour. You may think that these things do not matter because you are dying, but Mr Hassan, I can assure you of one thing. You are not dead yet. Life is long, longer than we think, even for you. It is not advisable to spend it in pain, of any sort.'

'If you're suggesting more medication, that's fine,' says Hassan. 'Medicate me up to my eyeballs. Put me in a damn coma; it'll pass the time.'

Smiling again, a professional smile used to put people at ease, disarming because it seems sincere, Dr Rahman makes another, final note, and then stands up. 'There are people here who are willing to be helped, Mr Hassan. It is better that I spend my time with them. If you do wish to talk, please just ask for me.'

When she leaves, Hassan feels oddly bereft. He realizes that he does want to talk after all, but not to her, this perfectly pleasant, perfectly ordinary woman, blessed with her ordinary cares. He wants to talk to the missing. He wants to tell his daughter that he is sorry that he let her go. He wants to ask his son to forgive him, and let him go in his turn.

Jazz

Changi Airport, Singapore

Jazz is on time, and Aruna's plane is disembarking just after his arrival. He gets a coffee and a doughnut at the cafe while he is waiting; he hesitates, and then goes back and gets one for her too. The chocolate iced one with the garish sprinkles, like a party cake. Well, it is sort of a party, thinks Jazz, Aruna is coming home; he should have hired a marching band to greet her on her arrival, rolled out a red carpet and found a winsome child in a frilly dress to offer her a bouquet of birds of paradise and tiger lilies, stems wrapped with golden ribbon. But, in the absence of all that, the doughnut will have to do.

It is funny, he thinks, how he casually described Aruna to June. Just a friend he was picking up from the airport. After all their years together, to have become reduced to being Just Friends despite everything. But what else could he have said? Ex-girlfriend sounded too flimsy and final, as though the relationship was over, when it was anything but, when it would never be really. And she had never been his wife or even his fiancée. It seems so stupid to him now that they had never got married; it might have made it easier to have stayed together; marriage was just a minor piece of legislation, a symbol, but to Singaporeans rules and symbols mattered. It was his fault; he'd wanted to, but he'd listened to the doctors; he should have known that no one could have decided what was best for Aruna and him apart from themselves. I never asked, he thinks to himself, I never even asked her. And then she ran away, and it was too late, too late, too late.

'My mum asked how you were,' said Jazz, coming back into the kitchen, where Aruna was reading the *Straits Times*, eating last night's takeaway for breakfast, as they had run out of cereal. He was still dressed only in his shorts, and Aruna just in a cotton vest and underwear, with a pair of red velvet slippers, embroidered with dragons and fake pearls, dangling from her feet.

'*Mee goreng*, or *nasi goreng*?' she offered companionably, pushing the plastic cartons of noodles and rice towards him. 'I've already had the chicken.'

'Damn, you know that's the only one I wanted,' he complained, looking hopefully at the empty container for some remaining scrap. 'You snooze, you lose,' said Aruna dismissively. 'You should have called your mum after breakfast, not before.' She scooped up some more noodles, and then asked, 'Did she ask how I was, in a

"How's your crazy girlfriend" kind of way, or a "How's your sweet old school friend" kind of way?'

'The latter,' admitted Jazz, 'I haven't told her about your condition, she'd only worry. She's been so ill recently with the treatment. If she doesn't respond they might need to operate.'

'Does that mean you haven't told her about us, either?'

Jazz shook his head, feeling disloyal to both of them, 'I wanted to, I really meant to after your dad passed away. But then there was the depression, and the bipolar thing, and the miscarriages, and telling her about us meant I'd have to tell her about all of that. Like I said, she'd only worry.'

'About you, you mean,' said Aruna harshly. She dropped her ceramic chopsticks with an angry clatter on the table and left the room.

'About both of us,' pleaded Jazz, following her. 'She's got cancer.'

'At least she's not dead,' said Aruna savagely, 'or mad.'

'Self pity doesn't suit you,' said Jazz quietly.

'Bullshit doesn't suit you,' she retorted. 'Why are we even pretending that we're going to get married? Our children keep dropping dead out of me, and I'm apparently as crazy as a coot. I'm not an idiot, Jazz. And neither are you. I can see that you just don't want to marry me any more.'

'You're right, I don't,' said Jazz, taking the wind out of her sails.

'Oh crap,' she said, her face collapsing into tears, as she sat down on the sofa. 'Of course you don't.'

'You don't get it,' said Jazz, sitting beside her and putting his arms around her. 'You know how much I love you, but the doctors think that the last thing you need is a wedding. The stress of it. We need to focus on you now, not on us. I've waited years for you, I can wait a bit longer.'

Aruna nodded through her tears. 'I know you're right. Damn it, I know you're right. I don't know, I just thought that getting married would be like a bloody great magic wand for us, and make everything OK; I wanted to believe in happy ever after.'

'I've always believed in magic,' said Jazz, wiping the tears from her face with his palm as though she were a child, 'and in happy ever after. It's how every one of my books ends.'

'With a kiss,' said Aruna. They looked at each other, and Aruna finally began to smile, and kissed him chastely on the lips.

'Or two,' said Jazz, and kissed her properly, pulling her back on the sofa to lie down with her, stroking her hair.

'I didn't tell you this before,' said Aruna, her face half muffled against his smooth chest. 'Dr Hudson says that I have an addictive personality.'

'Addicted to what? You barely drink, or smoke,' objects Jazz.

'To my work, but mainly to you,' she said, her voice carrying a rueful note of laughter. 'And soon to the meds, if I'm not careful. I wonder if that's how I've managed the bipolarity for so long; I've drowned it in addictions. Like burning your hand to suppress a migraine.'

'Sometimes I think the quacks are just looking for problems when there aren't any there,' said Jazz. 'I'm addicted to my work too. And I'm definitely addicted to you. But they're not labelling me with a mental condition. Ten years ago they'd have just said that you had a bit of a breakdown with your dad's death, and that would have been the end of it.'

Aruna looked at him solemnly, and kissed him again. 'I love you, you know.'

'What was that for?' Jazz said with pleased surprise.

'Because you believe in me. You always have. You believe that I'm all right, that we're all right after all. And it makes me want to believe it too,' she said.

Jazz sees activity at the arrivals side of the hall, and half strolls, half runs across. Everyone who comes through the doors is moving off quickly, trundling large cases on trolleys, or weighed down by unwieldy backpacks; they are all overloaded, they all have somewhere to go. But there, hesitating towards the back, is a figure that is burdened by nothing but a flimsy handbag and a light jacket, agitated and trembling, with all the substance of a sparrow. He sees her as a stranger might, thin, straggle-haired, inhabited by a distress that makes her almost ugly, and this ugliness moves him terribly, it moves him almost to tears; it makes her his secret. 'Jazz,' says Aruna, but he just stays there, and so she walks towards him, and then she is standing in front of him. 'Jazz,' she says, again.

Aruna

Changi Airport, Singapore

Aruna stands before Jazz, and gazes at him with an intimacy as great as touching. The handsome, high-cheek-boned face she knows as well as her own, the dip of his philtrum, the curve of his chin. The hair kept fashionably untidy from mild vanity. The slimness of his hips, the slimness of his whole blade-like body; the new definition in the sculpted muscles of his arms that flow under his smooth, dark skin. He is flickering with inconsistent energy, blazing like a star. She is unsure if he is going to hold her, or strike her: she is unsure which she deserves; she is unsure which she would prefer. She stands there, trembling and light-boned, like a bird ready to take flight, waiting for his decision. She sees him make it. She closes her eyes, remembering: a star, a bird.

'Welcome home, Rooney,' he finally says, and Aruna feels a raw sob rip through her body and escape. Jazz steps towards her, and they hold each other with the ease of two people who have never forgotten how, who know every hollow and curve of each other too well, faces buried in the other's neck, tears dripping over shoulders, so close that nothing, not even air, is between them. She does not know if they are feeling sorrow or ecstasy as they fill each other's arms, she does not know if they are giving comfort or receiving it. All Aruna knows, at this moment, is that they are living in a fragile world, and that they are so fragile themselves, they could be blown to the skies with just a gust of wind.

Some months after their third miscarriage, Jazz and Aruna went to see a play. A Jacobean tragedy which was relevant to the syllabus she was due to tutor, which had been publicized as ''*Tis Pity*', as the full title, ''*Tis Pity She's a Whore*,' was considered rather too racy and offensive.

'What's it about?' said Jazz, as they took their seats. Aruna looked at him with a mix of affection and impatience, wondering why he hadn't asked before; she supposed he'd been persuaded by the title alone.

'Star-crossed lovers meet horrible deaths, I think,' she replied. 'Sorry to sound vague but I haven't read Ford yet. He was writing about the same time as Shakespeare.'

As the play unfolded, it turned out that the star-crossed lovers were in fact brother and sister, intent on their incestuous relationship. As they came out of the play, Aruna was unusually quiet. 'What's up?' asked

Jazz. 'Normally you're mouthing off about the staging the moment we leave a production.'

'It was just so inappropriate – they were brother and sister, and they knew it, and they still pursued each other,' she said, glancing at the notes she had scribbled on her programme, ' "'Tis not, I know, my lust, but 'tis my fate that leads me on . . . Nearness in birth or blood doth but persuade a nearer nearness in affection." They tried to excuse it, justify it even. It's just disgusting.'

'That's the bit you find disgusting?' questioned Jazz with amusement. 'For God's sake, the brother walked in at the end with her bloody, dripping heart on a dagger.' He strolled on. 'It looked real, I suppose it was a pig's heart or something. You know, I had no idea that Jacobean plays were so exciting, we should look up some others . . .' He stopped, as Aruna had stayed back where she was, looking at him in horror.

'What?' he said.

'I can't believe we've been so stupid,' she said. 'It's been so obvious; it stares us in the face every time we look in the mirror.'

'What are you talking about?' asked Jazz calmly. He didn't seem too alarmed, as he had got used to Aruna's mood swings; they had been worst while she was trying to conceive and during her brief pregnancies, as she had been advised to stop taking her medication. Aruna had been encouraged to accept her changeable moods, as it was possible that she would never be completely free of them, even now she was back on her regular prescription;

she joked with Jazz that she was like the little girl with the little curl; some days she was very, very good, and some days she was horrid.

'I'm going home,' she said.

'Well, yeah, we're both going home,' said Jazz, 'unless you wanted to get a drink on the way.'

'I meant my place,' said Aruna. 'Don't follow me.'

A couple of hours later, Aruna heard Jazz knocking on her door. 'Rooney,' he called out, 'I'm not following you, honest, I've just brought you your meds. I'll leave them here, OK?'

Aruna opened the door, looking a tearful mess, just as he had started to walk away. 'Come in,' she said, but she pushed him away when he tried to kiss her hello. Jazz walked into her barely lived-in apartment, which they mainly used for storage, and stopped short, taken aback at the mess; she had ransacked all their family albums, the photos were scattered all over the floor, but she had ordered some in pairs like she had been playing some bizarre game of snap. 'Look,' she said.

She pointed to the first pair of photos, baby photos of each of them. And then to the pairs of photos from toddlerhood, and then schooldays, and so on. Jazz stared at them blankly, clearly wondering what was meant to be so significant. 'I don't get it,' he said eventually.

'You've been as blind as me. We only saw what we

wanted to see, what our parents wanted to see. Look, for Christ's sake, look!'

'Well,' said Jazz, looking again at the shots to try and work out what had got her so worked up. 'I suppose we look kind of similar as babies, don't we? Can't tell which is which, really. But all babies look the same, don't they?'

Aruna looked at him from the sofa, where she had curled her knees up into her chest, hugging them with distress. 'You keep saying things like that, Jazz, and it's just not true. All babies don't look alike, all Bengalis don't look alike. We look alike, that's the point. We've always looked alike.'

'I still don't get it,' said Jazz.

'Jazz, you idiot, can't you see that we're related? We must be.'

Several days later, Aruna still hadn't come home. 'This is ridiculous,' said Jazz, visiting her in her apartment again, where she clearly had barely been eating. 'Look, if you're not coming home, I'm going to have to move in here. You're not looking after yourself.'

'I'll come home when you make the call,' said Aruna.

Jazz lost his temper, 'Rooney, my mother is possibly dying from cancer. I am *not* going to call her up and ask if she or Dad had an affair which somehow resulted in you and I being related. Don't you think they'd have mentioned something by now?'

'Fine, just tell her you're screwing me, and see what she has to say about it,' said Aruna sharply.

'Rooney, I don't want to be rude here, but you really are acting like a nut. I'm not upsetting Amma, that's final. It's not your decision to make. Just move back in and we'll sort this out. It's just another weird paranoid episode, that's all, when you think that the whole world's conspiring against you. We should never have seen that stupid play.'

'How will we sort it out?' asked Aruna, raising her head.

'I don't know – talk to the doctors?' suggested Jazz.

To his surprise, Aruna nodded, quite sanely. 'OK, that seems sensible,' she said. 'But we're not sleeping together until we speak to them.'

'Fine,' said Jazz, obviously relieved at her capitulation, at the start of her swing back to normality. 'That's just fine.'

Unfortunately, the doctors were less sensible than they'd hoped. 'You know, I thought about mentioning it before,' said Dr Hudson, 'but I didn't want to trouble you unduly. The likeness is remarkable.'

'But that doesn't mean anything, does it?' interrupted

Jazz crossly. 'Does it?' he insisted when the doctor didn't answer.

'It's not my area of expertise, but you'd be surprised how often it happens, that people are related and don't realize it. It's a small island, Singapore, when all's said and done. And the Bengali community here is a pretty tight one. And with family traditions and saving face and whatnot, sometimes babies get adopted and brought up by people who aren't their natural parents. If the mother was a young girl who's got in trouble, and wants to get on with her life. And with fertility treatment too, the possibilities are endless. There was a recent case in the West of a brother and sister who got married, had five children, and didn't have a clue for twenty years. No ill effects on the children whatsoever.'

'What would we do if we wanted to find out?' asked Aruna.

'The simplest thing to do would be to talk to your parents,' said the doctor, 'They'd probably know if it was a possibility.'

Aruna looked at Jazz, and replied, 'We can't talk to our parents. Mine are dead, Jazz doesn't really speak to his dad, and his mum is apparently too ill to ask.'

'So, a DNA test, then' said the doctor cheerfully. 'Not cheap, but perfectly straightforward.'

122

A couple of weeks later, as Jazz and Aruna waited for the results of their DNA testing in the doctor's office, Aruna felt ridiculously optimistic. 'I'm so glad that we're sorting this out once and for all. That it'll be over and done with. It's been driving me crazy.'

'Yeah, and me,' said Jazz. 'Does this mean that we can finally get laid tonight?' he added jokily.

'It's so dumb when I think about it. If we were really related, of course we'd have known. Our parents would have said. There's no way that they couldn't know, is there?'

'None at all,' agreed Jazz. 'You know, you should have enjoyed being mistaken for my sister while you had the chance. In a few years' time, you're more likely to get mistaken for my mother.'

'Shut up,' retorted Aruna. 'I don't think you'll ever grow up. You'll just grow old.' Jazz laughed, and dropped a kiss affectionately on her shoulder.

The doctor came in, and smiling nervously, told them that he had the results, and assured them that they were completely private and confidential. 'So it shouldn't matter what you wish to do afterwards,' he said. 'You shouldn't feel that you have to change your plans.'

'What's that meant to mean?' asked Aruna apprehensively, her bubble of optimism disappearing.

'The results are incontrovertible, Miss Ahmed, Mr Ahsan. You certainly are related. We redid the test twice to be sure.'

There was a silence, and then Jazz asked quietly, 'How? How closely?' The doctor shuffled through the report nervously, and Jazz shouted, 'I asked how closely? Like cousins?'

'Closer than that, I'm afraid,' said the doctor. 'Half-siblings, sharing a parent. Sharing a father, but you could have guessed that; with only three months between you, you're too close in age to have had the same mother.' He looked nervously at them. 'Like I said, these results don't leave this office. If you wanted to carry on with your plans, get married. No one would object. Another pregnancy might be difficult in ethical terms; but there are other possibilities, a donor egg, a donor sperm, adoption. And if you did decide not to use those options, and you carried to term, Miss Ahmed, it's perfectly possible that you'd have a healthy child with no long-term problems.' He saw the two of them, shell-shocked, and said, 'I'll give you a moment.'

Aruna said nothing for a while, she just sat there tapping her fingers, while the deep black cloud of the disorder that always inhabited her, lurking under her skin like a recurrent virus, fed on her distress and bloomed back into being, filling her to the extremities, her fingers and toes, leaking out of her nose, ears and mouth, creeping along her hair follicles. It collapsed the walls of her flesh once more, and became the world around her. 'You were right not to have asked your mum,' she said at last.

'What?' asked Jazz in a daze, not understanding.

'It would have broken her heart. Even if it wasn't her. Even if it was your dad who slept with my mum. Even if it turned out that we were both adopted from some godforsaken village. It would have broken her heart to know what's happened to us.' Aruna got up, and picked up her handbag. 'I'm going now, Jazz,' she said. 'Take care of yourself, please.'

'Don't just go, Rooney,' pleaded Jazz. 'You heard what he said. We can still be together, we can still have children, get married, everything. No one in the world needs to know. I'll marry you tomorrow if that's what you want.'

'You never even asked me,' said Aruna, not accusingly, just with sadness and regret. 'And now it's too late.'

When Jazz got home, Aruna wasn't there. She wasn't at her apartment either. She wasn't at work the next day. She had simply disappeared. She hadn't waited to say goodbye, but had just spread her wings and flown.

In Changi Airport, Jazz and Aruna finally disentangle themselves, and he hands her the chocolate doughnut with sprinkles, 'Like I said, welcome home.' He gestures towards her tiny frame. 'You look like you should eat a bagful of these, you're way too thin.'

'You've been working out,' Aruna says, glancing again at his upper arms, feeling a bit stupid for saying something so trivial.

'Just a little,' admits Jazz, 'just to keep up. And you?'

'No, I haven't been keeping up, or working out. I haven't worked out at all,' she says with irony.

'I can tell,' he says, touching her face with affection, just lightly, tracing the cheekbones that they share, the enormous haunted eyes. 'You look awful.'

'You look wonderful,' replies Aruna, looking at her beautiful brother-lover-friend.

He adds quietly, 'I've missed you. But you know that.'

'You know I've missed you too,' she says, looking down at their hands, still linked together.

'I want you to tell me why,' he asks at last.

'Why I left? You know why.'

'Not that,' says Jazz. 'I want to know why you came back.' His face is shining with so much cheap hope that Aruna can no longer look at him. She guesses the words he wants her to say, the compelling, heartbreaking words, For you. I came back for you. But this is only part true. After the joy of holding him in her arms, she suddenly wants a drink and a cigarette more than she wants anything else in the world; more than she wants this moment, even. She realizes that running away really is the easy part; it is coming home that is hard.

Hassan

Kuala Lumpur General Hospital, Malaysia

Hari Hassan is relieved when indifferent Malay Nurse enters his room for the routine check-up, rather than the other one whose kindness seems to have led inexorably to her engaging with him, to her interfering. He is quite sure that even if he is writhing in agony and speaking in tongues, Malay Nurse would simply check his pulse, administer a mild sedative, and let him get on with it. No psychobabble for her, no imposition of cheerful golfers and softly spoken middle-aged women in beige suits. A cheerful young student, one of those volunteering at the hospital, pops in with a leaflet while Nurse is replacing his drip. 'Hello Hari,' says the student overfamiliarly, 'Are you going to come to the movie showing tonight? We could arrange for you to be wheeled down to the room. We're trying to drum up interest, as no one turned up last week. This time we're making popcorn as a bribe.'

'Mr Hassan could choke to death on popcorn,' says Nurse pragmatically, dismissing him, and the student looks slightly hurt and leaves. Thank you, Nurse, thinks Hassan, for making decisions for me, for scaring people away. I know you'd be perfectly willing to let me die, but just not on your watch, not on your shift. As the disease slides deeper into Hassan, inhabiting his legs so he no longer has the use of them, into his chest and throat so eating and swallowing are now difficult and soon talking will be too, it takes hold of him with a muscular, personal embrace, gripping him hard enough to kill little pieces of him, like cold fingers inching along his flesh. Hassan has had dreams sometimes where he has been placed in his coffin, his body shrunk to nothing, his skin stretched across the fleshless bone, his eyes lidded, his cadaverous smile fixed by the embalmer, and people pass and pay respects, shuddering at the horror of his mummy-like, reptilian form, as though he has regressed centuries, as though he has just evolved and crept slimily from the sea, and no one notices that he is still there, hidden inside the body, screaming silently for someone to hear him, to notice that his dry little heart is still pumping red blood to the strangled veins. I'm still here, he cries without moving his lips, pinned invisibly into place over his teeth, I'm still here in these paper walls, caged in my bones. He continues to cry out as the silk-lined coffin lid is shut over his face, as he hears the earth pound on him from above. When he has this dream, Hassan wakes to feel grateful for practical Malay Nurse, as he knows that she alone would not walk by him with creeping sentiment, but would look at his desiccated remains without affection, and efficiently check his pulse. She alone will make sure that he is dead before he is gone.

The student is back again already; this time with a little flyer he has probably made himself on his laptop. 'Forgot to give you this,' he says amiably to Hassan, 'Has all the films we're planning to show this month, and a section for suggestions.' He adds, 'It's a shame you can't come tonight,' looking reproachfully at Nurse, who ignores him. 'It's a real classic.'

'What is it?' asks Hassan despite himself. For some reason, at the word 'classic' he has a sudden image of the *Gone with the Wind* movie poster, that had been everywhere in Calcutta at the beginning of the war. He remembers how the Indian artists had somehow done something to Clark Gable's eyes and eyebrows and skin, that made him look like an Indian himself, as he hovered over a snowy-white Vivien Leigh.

'*Thelma and Louise*,' says the student.

'Oh,' says Hassan in bald disappointment. The student hovers, as though about to justify his choice, but a cough and a glare from Nurse send him from the room, and this time he doesn't return.

'No letters today?' Hassan asks Nurse hopefully.

'No letters today,' repeats Nurse flatly.

'It's just that yesterday one was left in the office,' Hassan begins to explain.

'No letters today,' says Nurse, with the exact same intonation. This tone reminds Hassan that there is no point hoping for the letter; the letter will or will not come whether he hopes for it or not. In fact, there is no point to hope, even; hope is just a veil we draw over future disappointment, Hassan reflects, remembering a line from one of his prose pieces on the war. Anwar had a rather chirpier take on the subject, and had written a snappy couplet, 'Better to deal with the hangman's rope, than live your life knotted up in hope.'

Hari Hassan's collection of poetry that followed Partition, *The Road from Hell*, was published to great acclaim; he received glowing reviews in the British and Indian press, and although the book was a commercial failure, it made his name in the subcontinent. He was praised for his subtle intertwining of external and internal conflict, for how he sought connections between the public and the personal while somehow managing to avoid the charge of being too 'political'. 'He twists steel swords and loaded guns into love knots,' said the *Manchester Guardian*; 'A young man in the service of anger, love and indiscernible truth,' said the *Times of India*. 'The prophet for our troubled times, his verse is a luminous guide to those who seek their own atonement,' said Anwar Shah, a journalist and lesser-known poet, in West Pakistan's *Tribune*.

In fact, it was his own atonement that Hassan sought. After Nazneen's burial, he buried himself. He refused invitations, received no one, and sat into the early hours, writing, writing, writing himself into insanity, and back again. He poured his violence, guilt, regret and self-loathing onto paper, and in doing so reflected the spirit of the age, as his countrymen reflected on the political botching of Independence, on the thousands killed during the flights of Partition, as Muslims and Hindus sought safety among their own kind. Hassan remained in Calcutta and remarkably, despite his best efforts, survived. When his house was burned to the ground, he gave Ruby enough money to return to her village in comfort, and went to East Pakistan, where he hid in the relative calm of Cox's Bazaar, in a bungalow near the long stretch of beach. He visited Chittagong on the way, and Mr Ali failed to kill him, or else failed to notice his presence there in the aftermath of all the troubles. He sat by Nazneen's grave for a little while; she's not here, he realized.

He looked for Nazneen instead in the eyes of every little girl he saw, being hurried along by their sari-clad mothers outside the ice-cream shop, riding in their rickshaws, walking to school. As the years passed, he looked for traces of her in the young women laughing with their friends, on their way to the beach, the park, the campus; they misinterpreted the hopeful questioning in his face, and either nudged each other with knowing giggles, or looked away with distaste. It was pointless to hope; he knew that he wouldn't find her, the parents had emigrated, the aunt wouldn't pass on their details and then passed away herself, and so the girl who carried his and Nazneen's blood could be anywhere in the wide world, a droplet floating in the Indian Ocean before him. The truth was, despite all his accomplished, self-obsessed verse, he did not know the road from hell, he did not know what would atone for the wrongs he had done Nazneen and their child. Death was an option, but it had thus far eluded him, and it seemed to him to be an excuse, an escape; it wouldn't make things right, it would only close his eyes. He kept himself busy, taking up journalism and finding himself in demand; with the civil unrest in the late sixties, he became overtly political at last, and wrote articles advocating Bangladeshi independence that were printed in the international press; he donated to charity, he was kind to children, animals and strangers. But he did not know whether he would ever again look in the mirror, and feel himself to be proud of what he saw; he did not know if he would ever again see himself as someone who was good.

One day, some twenty years after Nazneen's death, he came home from walking along the beach, and found Anwar seated on his veranda in a kameez so blindingly white in the sunshine that he might have been an angel. 'My dear old chap,' Hassan said, his eyes bright and swimming with too much sun and emotion, and he stumbled blindly onto the veranda, to hold his best friend, 'it's been so long.' He was doubly touched, as it was a dangerous time for a West Pakistani to be visiting; especially a military man, which Anwar now was, having given up writing after his patchy success. Civil war was looming, and everyone knew it.

Anwar held him close, comforting him as though he was a child. 'I have your last letter, Hari,' Anwar said. 'I hope it's not too late for you, because I think I may have found you a road out of hell.'

Jazz

Holland Village, Singapore

Jazz follows Aruna as she opens the door to her old apartment. She flicks switches experimentally, relieved that the electricity is still connected. 'I'll just have a quick shower,' she says, 'and we'll talk.'

'You could have come to my place,' says Jazz.

'I didn't want to have to make small talk with your girlfriend,' says Aruna, 'and besides, this is where I live.'

'She'd be at work, by now,' says Jazz, secretly pleased that Aruna doesn't want to see June. That has to mean something, doesn't it? He adds, 'I thought you'd have rented out this place, after all this time.'

Aruna shrugs, 'I didn't leave it in good enough condition to rent out. I let a colleague from the campus stay here for a couple of months this year, though. She paid me enough to cover some of the running costs, and clearly left it in a better state than I did.'

She goes to her bedroom and rummages through her wardrobe, pulling out underwear and some clean clothes.

Jazz sits on the bed, and then realizes that he is no longer someone who sits on the bed while she goes through her clothes, and that he is intruding. 'I'll leave you to it,' he says awkwardly. It occurs to him that in all his books, when his attractive couples race around the world and through disasters, that he never lets them stop long enough to change underwear; it seems an enormous oversight and he is amazed that no one has mentioned it to him before. No one performs heroic deeds in yesterday's underwear. 'I won't be long,' she says. 'Make yourself at . . .' she pauses and corrects herself, 'I mean, make yourself comfortable.'

Jazz goes to the kitchen, and checking the cupboards for green tea, puts on the kettle. He notices that the tea is the same brand that he buys; it is very likely the same packet that he bought two years ago, before they received the results. He doesn't know why it should make him feel so upset, that a foil packet of tea can survive the tests of time when they have not.

Aruna joins him soon after; he remembers that she was always quick at these sorts of things, unlike June who spends hours, quite literally hours, primping in the bath. 'You don't know how hard it is to look this good,' June has a habit of saying, and he's never quite sure if she's joking. Aruna's hair is dripping down her back, and like him she is still wearing yesterday's jeans. Her feet are bare, and her unpainted toenails gleam. She has beautiful feet, he thinks with a pang of longing, the skin smooth and uncallused because she almost never wore heels; her feet seem barely larger than his hands. Her slim legs in her too-baggy jeans, her slightly sharp collarbones, and the curve of her eyebrows; alone in this room, everything about her is suddenly breathtaking.

'You've got about a foot too much hair,' Jazz says, trying to cover his discomfort, and passes her a cup of tea.

'Thanks,' says Aruna, accepting it. 'I haven't had my hair cut in ages; I just can't be bothered with it. It's a London academic thing: there's something heroic about not bothering about how you look, as long as you look carelessly good. It's considered a bit distasteful if you put too much effort into something, unless it's a wedding or a ball. If you wear too much make-up, you're either very young, or a bit of a slut.' She blows across the tea, and then sips it carefully. 'This tea's great.'

'I only buy the best,' says Jazz unthinkingly, and sees Aruna stiffen, as she realizes that it really is Jazz's tea. Well, what does she expect? thinks Jazz with a flash of irritation. Does she think that she can come back here after just skipping out, and expect that all signs of what we were would have mysteriously vanished? Does she really think it's that easy to get rid of someone? He sees Aruna's hand shaking so badly that she has to put the tea down, as she splashes it over herself; she is shaking all over, in fact.

'Rooney, are you all right?' he asks, stupidly, as he can see that she isn't.

'Of course I'm not,' she snaps back.

Jazz looks at her again, annoyed that he hasn't realized this sooner, 'You're not taking your meds, are you?' He is suddenly furious. 'Why isn't that husband of yours making sure you take them?' he storms. 'How long have you been off them?'

'Oh, months and months, and stop shouting, you're making my head hurt,' says Aruna in a matter-of-fact voice. 'I don't need them, anyway.'

'Why are you shaking like that if you don't need them?' argues Jazz.

'Because what I really need now is just a fucking, great, big drink,' she snaps back, holding her head in her hands. 'I said stop shouting, I've got enough voices in my head without you raising the volume.' She looks up at Jazz, and confesses mockingly, 'My name is Dr Aruna Ahmed Jones, and I'm almost an alcoholic.'

'Oh, Rooney,' says Jazz sorrowfully.

'You can lose the pity face, I haven't seen that in two years, and you know what? I haven't missed it. Just find me a drink,' mutters Aruna.

Jazz goes to the cupboard, and after some rummaging, comes back with a glass and a bottle of red, dusky liquid.

'What's that?' she asks suspiciously.

'Cherry brandy. We used to keep it for Singapore Slings, remember? It's the only thing left – your colleague must have cleared out the booze.'

'Crap,' says Aruna, unconvinced by the merits of

cherry brandy, as she pours out a few fingers. 'Oh well, cheers.' She raises her glass to Jazz, and downs it in a couple of gulps.

'Better?' asks Jazz.

'A bit,' says Aruna.

'Why doesn't your husband keep you on your meds?' asks Jazz again, still angry that Aruna's care has been so poorly handled by the oaf she married. 'How could he let you stop taking them?'

'Let?' questions Aruna wryly, raising her eyebrows at Jazz, as though his implication that she needed looking after was both unflattering and inappropriate. 'He's not my keeper, and he doesn't know I need them. I've never told him about the bipolar thing, so he just thinks that I'm wacky and interesting, and occasionally a bit of a bitch,' she says lightly.

'What?' says Jazz in shock. 'How could you not tell him?'

'I've only known him for a year and a half; it's not as though I've ever had an episode with him that needed to be explained. Besides, I don't have to tell him everything. I don't know him well enough to, I suppose.'

'So why did you marry him, then?' asks Jazz, still confused.

'Because he asked,' she says simply. 'Because he wanted to.' Perhaps she doesn't mean to, but it sounds like an accusation.

'You know that I wanted to,' Jazz replies, hurt by her implication. 'You know that nothing's changed for me. I still want to take care of you, and be there for you. I'd marry you tomorrow, I really would.'

'How romantic. Unfortunate that you're my brother and that I'm already married. Apart from that, we're clearly made for each other, aren't we?' replies Aruna scornfully, pouring herself another cherry brandy.

Jazz sighs. 'So, if you didn't come back for me, what did you come back for?' Aruna refuses to meet his eyes; he is not sure he believes that she didn't come back for him; he is not sure that she believes it either. He sees Aruna start to tremble again, just slightly, and asks, 'Any other addictions I should know about?'

Aruna shakes her head, 'I'm not a junkie, not any more. I smoke, though, pot and cigarettes, they help.' She looks at Jazz, helplessly, staring at him with a desperate hungry confusion, that he's never seen on her before, the sort of look that someone dying of thirst would give a tall glass of water. She looks around the flat, and when her gaze flickers to the bedroom, she leaps up. 'Nope, no more addictions you need to know about,' she says. 'Let's get out of here.'

Jazz takes her to a local coffee bar, where she can smoke outside, and asks her again, 'I need to know, Rooney. What did you come back here for, if it wasn't for me?'

'There was something in a book, that last book you gave me,' she says. 'I've got it here. And something else;

I think what's been really tearing at me is not knowing, not knowing how or why it happened. My parents are gone, but I wanted to speak to yours.'

'You know I barely spoke to my father,' says Jazz. 'And I don't speak to him at all now.'

'But your Amma,' starts Aruna.

'Amma's dead,' says Jazz flatly. He looks at her closely. 'She died just after you left. You really didn't know? I emailed you.'

'I closed my old email accounts,' says Aruna. 'Oh, God, Jazz, I'm so sorry. She was in remission when I went, they said she had years left.'

'She did,' says Jazz harshly. 'She died in a fire at home. My father never loved her, he neglected her for years. They practically lived separate lives. I think she died because of him.'

Jazz had wanted to go after Aruna, but he had no idea where she was. He had stupidly assumed that she'd come back in a few days after she'd had some time to herself; even as the weeks turned into months, he still thought that she'd return. She had a life here in Singapore, she had a partner, a job, an apartment, friends; people didn't just walk out on their lives, did they? But Aruna wasn't like other people; she wasn't mad, or insane, however much she bitterly claimed that she was, rather she was astounding, but unstable. He could only hope that the swinging pendulum of her moods would balance itself, that whatever urge had made her leave would become an equal and opposite urge compelling her return, to where he would be waiting. He didn't tell his parents about Aruna's exit; he remembered her last words to him and knew she was right. And besides, his mother's well-being plummeted shortly afterwards; not her physical health, as she had been given good news, it seemed she was in remission, but her mental state. Having prepared so long for death, it was as though she seemed to have no idea how to live; she carried on like a walking ghost, a survivor of a nuclear accident who carried the promise of dying within her. She had once had her own vocabulary, as precise as poetry, all to do with the concerns of wifehood, motherhood, the beauty of domesticity: car pool, pooris, dry cleaning, lemon drizzle cake, cotton underwear, suncream, lampshades, furniture polish, ironing, beef satay, Harpic, bath sponges, bedlinen, apron, dinner party. But now she left these words scattered behind her for someone else to pick up and make use of. Instead she got up in the morning, washed, applied day cream and powdered her nose from habit; and then she simply waited until the evening, barely eating except as a distraction, toying with a few spoonfuls like a fussy toddler, before washing off her powder, applying her night cream and going back to bed. She let life happen to her, as though it was just one more burden, one more trial to get through. She lived only for Jazz, but even this was painful; he was aware when he visited that she was performing for him, putting on the costume of a normal life, saying her expected lines, but slowly and awkwardly as she had got out of practice; a stupid play in which she parodied herself, and both of them knew it.

His mother's distress shone a harsh and unflattering light on his parents' marriage; Jazz spoke little to his father, and found he had less and less to speak to him about once his parents had moved back to KL. As a boy he had adored him and craved his approval, but as he grew up he found that he didn't respect him, simply because it became obvious to Jazz that his father did not love his mother. Jazz supposed that theirs was an arranged marriage – his father was years older than his mother – and that neither had been delighted with the deal. But whereas his mother had always done her best to make him happy, his father had remained distracted and distant, or worse, indifferent. He wasn't cruel to Jazz's mother, he was tolerant and even kind, he complimented her on her cooking and on her many small achievements around the home, but without a trace of sentiment or real affection; she might as well have been the housekeeper.

Jazz's last conversation with his father was a heated argument. 'She needs something to live for, Baba. Can't you see that? She survived cancer and now she's thinking what's the bloody point of it all.'

'I can't do any more than I'm doing, Jazz,' his father had said wearily. 'I can't do any more than I've done. She's comfortable, isn't she? She doesn't want for anything. And I don't know what the bloody point of it all is, either. If you ever find out I'd be delighted to hear it.'

'I don't know how you can be so flippant about it, Baba. She's dying, can't you see that?'

'We're all dying Jazz. We're all dying anyway, faster or slower is just a matter of perspective,' his father said.

'Just shut up, Baba. Amma has devoted the last thirty years of her life to you, you selfish old windbag, and now all you can come up with is stupid intellectual witticisms,' snapped Jazz. 'She needs more than that from you, she needs to know that she hasn't wasted her life. That it meant something, and still means something. That her marriage means something.'

'I'm exceedingly grateful to your Amma,' said his father, 'for the last thirty years. And for you. She knows that.'

'I don't think she knows that you love her; don't you think that would have made a difference?'

'I've looked after her,' began Jazz's father, but Jazz just interrupted angrily.

'That's not what I said.'

'I'm sorry, Jazz. I've never lied to her and I'm not lying to you. I don't love your mother. We were never about love, and she knows that too.'

143

Jazz looked at his father, open-mouthed with horror. 'You never even cared a bit about her, did you? You dried-up old bastard. You'd let her wither away in your house, while you just carried on, without giving a crap.'

'Of course I don't want her to wither away. When the time comes, I hope it's quick. I hope it's quick for me too. There's nothing worse than living in pain,' said his father quietly and practically.

Jazz looked at him in disgust and walked out of the house. After calming himself down for a few minutes, he went back into the kitchen, where he knew his mother was sitting, waiting for him to say goodbye. As he approached, she gave him that bright, artificial smile, heartbreaking in its brave pathos. 'I love you, Ejazzy-Jazz,' she said, reverting to his childhood nickname unthinkingly, and running her hand over his head to comfort him, as though Jazz had just run up to her in short trousers with bleeding knees from a careless fall. 'Please don't be hard on your father. We owe him a great deal; and if it wasn't for him, I would never have had you.'

'We don't owe him anything,' said Jazz harshly, and then regretted it when he saw the look on his mother's face.

'You need to understand, Jazz, that your Baba and I are from a different generation than you. You expect the world, and you have the right to. I was taught to expect nothing, and your father gave me more than I thought I would ever have. My own home. Comfort. Respect.'

'You deserve more, Amma,' said Jazz, angry at his

mother's browbeaten complicity, at her taking his unworthy father's side.

'I was never certain that I deserved even that,' said his mother, with the baffling humility of a slave questioning her right to freedom. Jazz shook his head, and tried to hide his fury; marriage to his father had broken his mother down over the years, and Jazz had let it happen.

'Take care, Amma, I'll visit soon. Next weekend?'

'Yes, darling,' said his mother with that brave and brittle smile; he left, but when he glanced back, just quickly, he saw that she had already let her face crumple into her backstage expression of listless despair.

A few days later there was an accident. Early in the morning, in the house left conveniently empty by his father, who had gone to Melaka to attend a lecture, there was a fire. It had apparently started in the kitchen where Jazz's mother had been sitting. She would have died quickly from the smoke, and her synthetic sari caught the flames and wrapped them around her in a sinuous embrace. The circumstances were suspicious, but it was ruled to be neither suicide nor murder, but simply, prosaically, accidental death. After the funeral Jazz never saw his father again, never answered a call and never replied to a letter; when his father was forced to go to hospital for his own rapidly failing health, Jazz vowed to himself that, for his father, it wouldn't be quick. Jazz was unsure whether his father had allowed his mother's death by shameful neglect or facilitated it with positive action, but he knew one thing: Hari Hassan Ahsan would live out every painful moment of life that had been denied his wife.

Aruna

Holland Village, Singapore

Jazz goes to sort out the bill, and as he walks away, Aruna tries to avoid watching him, and staring at his body too appreciatively. She is relieved that they are somewhere public, as she had been almost overwhelmed by the feeling of helpless desperation she had in her flat. (Home, she reminds herself. This isn't the flat, like the one in Bethnal Green, east London. This is her home, never mind that she'd not lived there for two years, and hadn't even bought the tea that was in the cupboards.) The wave of emotion and need had been so strong, a physical tugging inside her, that it had frightened her; she is frightened even now, when she realizes how easy it would have been to succumb to it, to sink drowning below the water, dragging Jazz with her, stealing the air from his lungs; Jazz still wanted to be with her, and all she had seen as she looked about the apartment was the kitchen table, the upstairs landing, the sofa, the armchair, the bath, the wall, the floor, and the bed, the bed, the

147

bed. The bed he sat on while she chose her clothes, a bed they once shared.

She bites hard on her lip, pulls out the book that Jazz had given her, and starts flicking through the pages to keep her mind from it. Then her phone starts ringing, and she answers it gratefully for the distraction, before she realizes that she already knows who is calling her. 'Aruna,' says Patrick, 'where the hell are you? It's two in the bloody morning and you're not home yet.'

'I've left,' Aruna says bravely. It occurs to her a moment later that it would have been a bit clearer to have said, 'I've left you,' and she doesn't know why she didn't.

'I can see that,' says Patrick crossly. 'I can see that by the fact that you aren't here. And when you ran off to see your friend, you left the place in a mess again. It was your turn with the dishwasher, remember, but your rancid porridge was still on the table when I got back; in another few hours it would have crawled off by itself. It's not exactly what I need after pulling a double shift.'

'You mean I'm not what you need after pulling a double shift,' retorts Aruna. 'So guess what, you don't have to put up with me any more.'

'Obviously I don't have to,' says Patrick, 'but I do, don't I? I guess I must like having you around.' His voice has moved from belligerence to tenderness so fluidly that Aruna can't tell where one ended and the other began. 'So when are you coming home?'

'I'm not,' she says, shortly.

'Of course you are; I can see that you've not taken

anything with you to stay away,' says Patrick sensibly. 'Is this about the argument we had yesterday? About the baby?'

'No,' says Aruna. 'I'm just not coming back.'

'Look, I'm so tired of fighting too,' he says. 'We'll just park it from now on. Let's just agree not to talk about that for a while – it's clearly freaking you out, and I don't want you getting upset.'

'Patrick,' says Aruna, wondering if there is some weird echo on the line, which means he doesn't actually hear a word that she is saying, 'I said that I've left. And I'm not coming back. Not today. Not tomorrow. I'm staying where I am.'

Patrick sighs, and says nothing for a moment. Her words hang in the air between them, like grey clouds heavy with rain, but then he recovers himself and says magnanimously, 'Look, that's fine.'

'Oh,' says Aruna, suddenly stunned by this unflattering capitulation. 'Oh, OK then,' she stammers, 'Thank you, I guess, for not making this too hard.'

'No problem,' says Patrick. 'It's absolutely fine. Stay with your friend for what's left of the night. Stay tomorrow if you must. Share a few bottles of white, have some joints, do whatever it is you usually do with your mates to get away from me and get some space. Bitch about me until the cows come home. Just come back the day after, please, because I'll be missing you.'

'Patrick,' starts Aruna, but he interrupts her.

'It's OK, really,' he says. 'Take care for now, I love

you.' He doesn't wait for her to say it back, because he knows that she has never made a habit of it; he seems about to hang up when he suddenly says, 'Oh, and the credit card company called about some flights to Singapore you booked. Just checking out the unusual activity on the account. We really need to talk about these sorts of things first; I know you like being impulsive, but they've cost the earth and I've got no idea when I can get away, so I hope they're flexible.' He clearly feels embarrassed for mentioning something as crude as money, as he says again, 'Love you,' and swiftly hangs up.

Jazz is back in his seat, 'So, that was him.'

Aruna looks at her phone, sitting on the table between them, 'Yes, that was Patrick.'

'Patrick,' snorts Jazz in disgust. 'I preferred him when he didn't have a name.' He taps his hand on the table, 'English, I suppose?'

'British,' corrects Aruna. 'His dad's from Wales.' There is a stiff moment of silence, as Jazz isn't sure where Wales is and doesn't want to care enough to ask.

'So what did he say?' asks Jazz eventually.

'Nothing much,' says Aruna. 'He doesn't seem to think that I've left him, although I was very clear on that point.' She suppresses an ironic laugh. 'I suppose we were never very good at communicating.'

'Clearly better than we were – you didn't even take your phone when you left me,' says Jazz. Aruna flushes because he is right.

'It's different,' she says. 'I had to get away from you,

from us. I was so sick in myself that I just felt dirty, all the way through. But I'm not escaping Patrick, and there's nothing wrong with him. He's a perfectly nice guy. He's so nice that he married me and wants to have children with me, without knowing me at all, really. I'm not getting away from him, I'm just coming home.'

Jazz picks up her phone, and Aruna realizes with embarrassment that the display has switched over to the photo that Patrick had loaded on when he first gave it to her. A shot from their wedding day, his arm protectively around her, looking ridiculously happy and proud. Her mouth is wide open in laughter, but she can't remember at what. Possibly at an inappropriate joke during the best man's speech, possibly at the absurdity of being a bride in a strappy white dress, holding roses in one hand, and a picture-perfect groom in the other. 'Big, isn't he?' says Jazz, looking closely at the picture. 'Tall, I mean. He really does look like a perfectly nice guy,' he adds, seemingly a little disappointed that he can't find something to fault. 'My turn, I suppose,' and he hands Aruna his own phone, with a photo of himself in shorts and June in a bikini, grinning to camera, with arms draped around each other, on the same stretch of beach that she and Jazz used to go to.

'Christ, she's gorgeous,' complains Aruna. 'How old is she? Twelve?'

'Twenty-one,' says Jazz. 'I said that you ought to appreciate me before I had my midlife crisis, and started dating women ten years younger than me.'

'And look at her tits,' continues Aruna, looking down at her own flat chest critically. 'I never had tits like that, except when . . .' She stops herself mentioning her second and third pregnancies, during which her chest had briefly inflated to hitherto unknown proportions, and just looks away, staring at the street outside the cafe.

Jazz realizes, and reaches across, taking her hands in unselfish sympathy. Glancing at him, she sees that he looks just as miserable as her at the memory. 'Maybe you should have got knocked up by your gallant English-man before you came home; then we could have been a family after all,' he says quietly. Aruna is unsure whether he is so quiet because he is being serious, or because he is simply sad.

I'm so tired of fighting, Patrick said, I hate all our bick-ering, he said, and yet he never seemed tired enough, or to hate it enough, to stop. They fought over everything, it seemed, but honestly, what did they have to fight over, after all? Most of their fights involved no Big Important Questions; they were about nothing so much as the trivi-alities of everyday life that happened to all couples. Some-times Aruna thought that their fighting, bickering, nagging, whining and arguing were all started deliberately by him, to fortify the reality of their relationship, as the fights were at least something that they shared. When it came down to it, they shared little else, as like most London couples they both worked a lot, and didn't spend that much time together; they had separate friends, separate lives. She liked it that way; he, possibly, liked it slightly less. The only other thing they shared was the urgent physical attraction that had brought them together in the first place, and which continued to bring them together late at night or early in the morning, on the kitchen table, the upstairs landing, the sofa, and anywhere else that her needy and hungry flesh could collide with his.

The Fight about Jealousy

'Hey darling, you're back. I'm just going out for lunch. I told you, already, didn't I?' said Patrick.

'No, but it doesn't matter,' said Aruna.

'What's up?'

'Nothing's up. I thought you were heading out?'

'Don't you want me to go?'

'Go, have a great time.'

'That sounded sincere. Don't you care where I'm going, or who I'm meeting?'

'Not if you don't care enough to tell me.'

'I'm meeting a gorgeous nurse who's just joined the hospital and who's completely got the hots for me.'

'And who wouldn't?' replied Aruna. 'So go, have a great time. Use protection.'

'Couldn't you just attempt a little jealousy? Just fake it to be polite, on occasion?'

'I might be a fake, sometimes, but you know I'm not a faker. And what would be the point?' said Aruna. 'If you were going to cheat, my being jealous is hardly likely to stop you. It might even encourage you.'

'As though I'd have the energy to cheat. When you insist on shagging every day and twice at weekends.'

'Besides, you're never even slightly jealous of me. When was the last time you asked me where I was going for lunch?'

'You seem to like being secretive and mysterious, so I try to let you. And I am jealous of you, I loathe it when you wear those leather trousers you've got, or short dresses in the summer.'

'Not wanting people to check out my butt or legs isn't the same as being jealous.'

'And besides, I trust you.'

'So, I trust you too.'

'I'm not so sure you do, not in the ways that count,' he argued.

'And now you're having a go at me for saying that I trust you. What's wrong with this picture?'

The Fight about Strangers

'Who was that suit you were talking to?' said Patrick.

'I don't know, some guy,' said Aruna.

'What were you talking about?' he persisted.

'Miró. I said that the first work showed influences of

Miró. The one with the woman, the bird, and the star –
I said that those symbols were part of Miró's artistic
vocabulary. He disagreed. And then I said that he ought
to go to the Miró Fundación in Barcelona. And he agreed.
And then you called me over looking like a wet weekend.
And I wouldn't have come if you hadn't managed to
score me a glass of Pimms.'

'You hate suits, why were you talking to a suit?'

'And I don't hate suits per se. I hate suits on you,' she
said, before adding, 'they don't *suit* you.'

'Ha-ha. I was wearing a suit the first night you slept
with me.'

'I only slept with you because I had to get you out
of it, it looked so awful,' she said. 'I thought you never
got jealous? So are you just annoyed, or something?
Because I spoke to someone at a gallery for all of two
minutes?'

'No, I just don't like the way you talk to strangers.
You do it everywhere, at a gallery, at the bloody bus
stop, at the supermarket.'

'Why does that bother you?'

'You talk to strangers like they're important,' he complained. 'Maybe it reminds me that we were strangers
when we met. You talk to strangers with more interest
than you ever talk to me.'

'I talk to you.'

'You've never once ventured a single opinion about
Miró to me. Ever. Or his artistic vocabulary. Or his Fundación in Barcelona. Go on, tell me about Miró.'

'Oh, shut up.'

'See?'

The Fight about Toilet Roll and Porridge

'When you finish the loo roll, would it kill you to put a new one out?' asked Patrick. 'It's hardly fun for me to have to hop halfway across the bathroom with my pants around my ankles.'

'What a charming image. And you say we never talk.'

'I mean really, would it kill you?'

'What's the big deal? You could have put one on before you sat down – that's what I would have done,' said Aruna.

'Yeah, because you'd have known that you'd already used up the last one.'

'If we left them all by the loo, like I said we should, it wouldn't even be an issue.'

'Well, I don't want to look at a bathroom with a dozen loo rolls littering up the floor,' muttered Patrick.

'You always exaggerate, it would be more like a couple stacked up by the wall.'

'We have cupboards you know, we're not students or savages. And you could put your porridge oats in the kitchen cupboard too, I have to put the packet back in every morning.'

'And I have to take it out again. Why can't you just leave it on the counter? I use it every bloody day, and you're always putting it away,' said Aruna. 'It's really annoying.'

'It's called tidying up.'

'So why don't you tidy the rest of the crap that we don't use every day, and leave me some space for my bloody oats, you selfish git? Look, an asparagus steamer? Why do we have an asparagus steamer on the worktop? When was the last time we ate asparagus, or steamed anything? And three glass jars of decorative pulses that we're never going to eat? And I don't even know what the fuck this thing is.'

'It froths milk. Would you calm down? I can't deal with this, Aruna. I'm just asking you to put your bloody porridge oats away. I do everything else around here.'

'No one asks you to, you complete and utter freak. Why are you making such a big deal about this?'

'Why are you?'

'I'm going out, I need some cigarettes anyway.'

'You walk out that door now, you can forget getting laid tonight,' said Patrick.

'I'll have more fun getting laid on my own. Porridge and toilet roll, for fuck's sake! Porridge and fucking toilet roll!'

The Fight about Being Aloof

'That was amazing. I mean, you're amazing,' said Patrick.

'Mmm, sweet of you to say. I aim to please,' replied Aruna.

'I doubt that, somehow. But you're still amazing.'

'You've mentioned that already, I think.'

'So, what's going on in there?'

'What?'

'I just asked you what you're thinking.'

'Are you kidding me?'

'No.'

'Nothing much,' replied Aruna. 'Why, what are you thinking?'

'I'm thinking that I'm very glad I married you, and that I love you very much.'

'Crap, that's a tough one to follow.'

'You could just tell me that you love me, too.'

'You know that's not me. You're the one who signs "Love Patrick" on notes to two-night stands or the postman or random people at work, and puts four kisses on every text message. I'm just not demonstrative that way.'

'You were plenty demonstrative just now. You know your problem?'

'I know several. Which did you have in mind?'

'You're emotionally unavailable. You act like you're on the other side of the world when you're here in my arms. You're so aloof, it's like you're scared of what would happen if you ever trusted someone enough to let them in, in case they might not like the real you behind all the mystery and smoke and mirrors.'

'Well, maybe I'm not emotionally unavailable. Maybe you're the one that's too needy.'

'There's nothing needy about expecting your wife to say she loves you. It's the most normal thing in the world.'

'But what if she doesn't? Or can't.'

'Oh, that's just great, Aruna. God, you're a bitch, sometimes! You couldn't even wait for the cuddle to finish without crapping on me from a great height. And the worst thing is that you don't mean it, you just want to push me away.'

'Where are you going?'

'Out. We've just shagged for an hour, God forbid we get *intimate*. God forbid we get *close*. Sometimes I haven't got a clue who you are, really.'

And Aruna said helplessly to the door that Patrick slammed behind him, alone and full of knotted imperfections, in a lost voice that he would never hear, 'Sometimes I haven't got a clue who I am, either.'

'I want to know what we are to each other, Jazz,' says Aruna. 'I need to know who I am. I need to know, and there's only one person left to ask.'

'I don't want to talk to him,' says Jazz. 'He doesn't deserve it.'

'It's not for him, Jazz. It's for us, for you and me. I let

my dad die without asking him the things that mattered; please don't make the same mistake.'

Jazz taps his hands on the table, an annoying habit she remembers, something that showed he was thinking. 'Do you fight with him?' he asks suddenly.

'What?' says Aruna, surprised. 'With Patrick? We bicker a lot. Yes, I suppose we do fight. I mean we did. Why?'

'We hardly ever fought, did we? We just agreed with each other straight away the moment either of us said anything. Even when there were things to fight about, after college, we never fought.'

'You're right, we didn't,' says Aruna, wondering why the thought of this should sting. It feels like a reproach. She pauses, and asks, 'Does this mean you're going to fight me on this? About going to see your dad in KL?'

Jazz looks at her ruefully, and shakes his head, as though in disbelief. 'Train, plane or car, Rooney?' he says eventually.

'I can smoke on the train, right?' she asks.

He nods, and for some reason this slight gesture has a silver thread of laughter laced into it, as though they are both agreeing to something inappropriate and daring, like the time they spat off a bridge into traffic when they were twelve years old. 'So train it is,' he says.

Hassan

Kuala Lumpur General Hospital, Malaysia

Hari Hassan is appalled at how he is able to while away a day doing nothing at all, folding himself in memories, some real, some invented, locking himself in them like a reflection behind glass. He receives visitors on occasion, who bring routine medical care and personal hygiene in their efficient wake, opening out his body like a deckchair or an umbrella, before folding it away again for storage, but he lets these things happen to him; he participates politely, and although they punctuate his day and he acknowledges the humiliation of his helplessness, he feels disconnected from them. He is disconnected from his own creaking body, as though his metallic, bright mind is racing freely around his insides, his ghost in the machine, like a steel ball in a children's toy maze seeking its exit. He has learned that staring at the wall or ceiling all day raises concerns among his carers, and so he occasionally puts the television or radio on, and tolerates the distraction of light and noise.

'You'll need to try harder,' Nurse says bluntly, seeing how little food he manages to eat, 'or we'll need to feed you with a tube soon.' Hassan shrugs inside, as moving his shoulders is difficult in his prone position, one more humiliation, one more delegation of responsibility for his body. His speech is beginning to fail, too. He knows by the extra look of concentration that people give him when he speaks; once it goes altogether, and he falls into silence, he suspects that others will begin to be more silent with him. And his engagement with the world will cease. For a man of words, this frightens him, a great deal more than death; 'I lived by words, and die without them,' he thinks to himself. Another little scrap of dog-gerel verse that he will never have a need to use.

Nurse tells him that Khalid Shah, Anwar's son, has called to say that he will be visiting that evening. Hassan is still able to sigh and look reproachful, and he does these well enough to show his feelings about this matter; it bordered on the disrespectful for Khalid to believe that Hassan would have even started to look at the diaries: did he think that the infirm and dying had nothing better to do with their time? Evidently not. 'There is only one thing duller than other people's dreams,' Anwar had once said, 'and that's other people's diaries.' Hassan feels some affection at this, and knows that his old friend would greatly regret the bother that his devoted son is putting him to. He asks Nurse to prop him up, and picks up the leather-bound books in his papery hands; the supple hide covering seems more vigorously animal and alive than his own translucent skin. He goes to the seventies, to the beginning of his and Anwar's parting of ways regarding Bangladeshi independence. But ironically, the first letter of this period, from Anwar to himself, is one of warm congratulations, on his unexpected and sudden marriage to Zaida Kamran, a woman of good family, but no longer in the first blush of youth. A perfect match for a fifty-something bachelor seeking a companion for his sunset years. 'I know that she will bring you happiness, Chief,' Anwar had written. 'And you have no idea of the joy that children will bring to your life.'

Hari Hassan's marriage was in fact arranged by Anwar, and the letter was something public rather than personal, something that could be appropriately shown to family and friends. Zaida Kamram was a cousin of Anwar's wife; her first marriage had ended in premature disgrace, as it turned out that her groom already had a wife and children in Dhaka, and had married her for her dowry. She was not considered especially attractive, and so after such bad luck her family had not attempted to find her another husband. Instead, she had remained in her family home, as an unpaid servant to her officious, intolerant parents, and as an unpaid nursemaid to her brother's various progeny. Her only business outside the home, and even this was frowned upon by her relatives, was that of assisting at charitable functions and hospital volunteering. It was therefore considered a minor miracle that in her early thirties, Zaida Kamran, having not altogether agreed with her family's decision to bury her alive at home for the rest of her years, found herself with child. Zaida was a kind woman, but she felt no kindness for her family, who had crushed every one of her hopes and dreams without consideration or explanation, and had not even allowed her to complete her basic schooling. She did not doubt for one moment that on hearing her news they would beat her half to death, until the child that lived inside her was crushed too, and pushed out in bloody pieces from her womb. And that then they would finish the job, or else keep her locked in the family home until either she or they died. In desperation she confided in her cousin, Meeru, whom the family never spoke to as she had had the bad luck to marry a man from the Punjab, who had become a military man with the hated West Pakistani army. Meeru confided her cousin's predicament to her husband, Anwar Shah. And Anwar, reading the latest letter from his dearest friend, about how his life had been empty since he had allowed the death of his one true love, and the loss of his only child, realized that he could redeem two souls at once, and save the life of an innocent child as well. He realized that he could help the world become a better place, and liked himself that day for knowing he would have a hand in it.

'It's a simple proposition, old chap,' Anwar said in Hassan's sober dining room, which was mercifully cool even in the baking midday heat. 'The family have no idea of the pregnancy as yet, but there's little time to waste. My wife will send a letter introducing you and suggesting the marriage, we'll say some rubbish about you needing companionship in your twilight years. Meeru will wax lyrical about your commitment to an independent Bengal and that you'll waive the dowry. You just have to make a visit and behave dour and respectable, and we'll seal the deal. They'll be glad to be rid of her; they know she hates them, and no wonder. It's a terrible world we live in that will condemn a young woman to that sort of life, and then condemn her again for daring not to accept it.'

'I don't know,' said Hassan helplessly. It didn't seem simple at all, it seemed as twisted as one of those Shakespearean plots that Nazneen had loved, and as ripe to end in tragedy.

'It will be a tragedy if you don't help her,' Anwar persisted seriously, with his disconcerting habit of reading Hassan's mind at precisely the right moment. 'You said you wanted a road out from hell, to expiate what happened to Nazneen and your daughter. Well, this is it. Whatever happened to Nazneen is going to happen to Zaida, or worse. This is your redemption, Hari, if you want to take the chance. You can look after this girl, you can be a father to her child.'

'But she's not Nazneen, and it's not my child,' said Hassan, who saw the sense in what Anwar proposed, and so was unsure exactly why he was still arguing.

'She was someone's Nazneen. And this is someone's child,' said Anwar. 'Zaida is refusing to talk about the father, but whoever he is, he doesn't seem to be in a position to help. Let's try to make right what went wrong, all those years ago. Save her, my friend, save yourself.'

Hassan knew that he had no choice. He couldn't live with the idea of refusing, and of perhaps reading a newspaper headline a few months later, of a young woman bludgeoned to death in the family home by 'robbers', or dying of mysterious internal bleeding, or found burnt to death and coated in kerosene in some inexplicable suicide. And so he took Zaida into his home, and treated her with the same kind of courtesy with which he had come to treat everyone. And when the child came, he was surprised that he wasn't in the slightest bit disappointed that it was a boy. They named him Ejaz, Anwar's middle name, and Hassan had to acknowledge that Anwar had been right in his letter – he really had had no idea of the joy that a child would bring to his life. His little Ejazzy-Jazz was an infant delight, with precocious speech and charming affection; 'Baba you so funny, Baba you so ridd-yik-ill-us!' he would cackle in fluent English when no more than three years old at Hassan's animal impressions, and at times Hassan couldn't believe that it wasn't his blood that was running in this creature's veins, that the scents of milk and soap and earth and occasionally astringent pee that drifted from the child weren't his to claim. He and Zaida were so pleased with Jazz that they tried to have more children, but it didn't work out. He was too old, he supposed, and she was no longer so young. He didn't think it mattered too much; he thought he was a good person when he caught his reflection in passing, in a shop window, upside down in a spoon, rippling in a rainy-season puddle; he had brought something to the world, he had fathered this boy more completely than the natural father could ever claim to. He thought, foolishly, that he would have his child forever.

It was during the Singapore years that Hassan first realized that they were losing their son, to his adolescence, to his school friends, to the new place that he frequently visited in the bright metropolis that was simply called 'out'. Hassan would glance questioningly at Zaida across the dinner table, and she would look back at him helplessly; there was no way to control this change, there was no way to avoid that the one thing that kept them together was slipping away. Zaida was still a kind, gentle woman, and Hassan was still a kind, gentle man, but there was no love between them and never had been. Their attempts at making love had been just that, brave and helpless attempts to create love from nothing, to replicate the feelings they should have had, and on occasion wished to God they did. As Hassan grew older and more belligerent, and more intolerant of their independent son, Zaida grew nervous in his presence. She was an excellent cook, and she started making persistent social arrangements around food, a favourite meal for him the next evening, a tea for neighbours next week, a dinner party next month, as though by tying up his future with her culinary promises, she could make sure that she remained a part of it; a modern Scheherazade, staving off her final sentence by leaving her edible stories half untold each night. She was waiting, he knew, for the time that he would say, 'We no longer need to be together, do we?' She knew that she would be provided for, there was no shame in divorce in the modern world. And yet he was fully aware that she was dreading this inevitable moment, the moment that would show everything before was a well-meaning fraud.

And it had not even taken divorce to show the fraud to their son; when Zaida received the diagnosis of cancer, Hassan was unable to show anything more than sympathy and a practical concern for her comfort and the quality of her treatment. In his own way, he cared for her; he was grateful for her loyalty to him, and he had never asked anything from her, apart from being a good mother to their son. He had not even presumed her fidelity, although he supposed that she had been faithful; he had never even asked her the name of Jazz's father. But he did not love her. That was the cold, stark fact of the matter. He never had. He never would. And his son began to hate him for this placid lack of hypocrisy; Anwar had been right in talking of the joy a child would bring to his life. But he had omitted to mention the misery of a child leaving his life; the creeping distress, like his creeping disease, of knowing that he was hated by the one he most loved, that he was being eaten away and erased from life and memory, simply for being who he was.

'Someone else called,' says Nurse, reading a note from the office. 'She said she was researching some academic paper, and that you might remember her. Dr Aruna Ahmed.'

'Dr Aruna Ahmed,' says Hassan questioningly, it is the title that confuses him for a moment; living in the hospital he sometimes forgets that not all doctors are medics. 'Rooney,' he quickly realizes, Jazz's school friend. Little Rooney, who had looked so much like him in their early teens that they might as well have been twins, with their skinny, coltish legs and their expressive hands. Rooney with the thick, straggly hair which his wife had used to tame into beauty, and the direct, questioning gaze. Of course, like Jazz, she would have grown up too; she had apparently earned a doctorate; he thinks that he might have known that already. Perhaps she had got married. Perhaps she had children of her own. 'Rooney, I mean, Aruna is coming to visit?' he asks.

'Tonight,' confirms Nurse, before leaving him with a crisp nod.

Hassan feels hope, that veil against future disappointment, rising like a song within him, like a star emerging from a misty sky. Aruna is coming; and he remembers from his Singapore years, that wherever Aruna used to be, just a few steps before or behind, was Jazz.

Jazz

Ekspres Sinaran Train, Singapore to Kuala Lumpur

Jazz and Aruna are sitting opposite each other on the afternoon train to KL, while Aruna blows smoke meditatively out of the open window, and picks at the masala dosa and fried fish in sour tamarind curry that Jazz had bought from a vendor at the station. Jazz had to drop his car back at his apartment, and was dismayed when Aruna suggested she just meet him at the train; he had no intention of letting her out of his sight, in case she fled as impulsively as she had returned. He insisted she ride with him, and when he parked, suggested she come upstairs, but she shivered and refused, as though the thought of being back in their home was too hard. He ran up swiftly to get his passport and a jacket, and after a moment's hesitation, pulled out a never-forgotten paper bag that he'd kept at the back of the kitchen cupboard, with all the rarely used condiments. This is the paper bag that he fingers uneasily in his pocket, while he stares at her profile, at her delicate ear with the inky dot of an old piercing on her lobe, at her thick hair getting whipped by the wind.

Aruna looks across at him, and catches his eye. 'What?' she asks. He wonders if he had been Patrick, whether she would have said it quite as accusingly. He realizes at that moment that she is still wearing her wedding ring; he had seen her fiddling with it, but had not really registered its significance before, thinking it was just a random bit of jewellery. He wonders if she hasn't taken it off because it means too much, or because it means so little. Perhaps she has just got so used to it on her hand, that she does not really register what it is, either. She fiddles with it again, twisting it slightly up her finger, so he can detect a narrow band of dampness beneath where it had been. He pretends not to have seen this slight gesture.

'Disgusting habit,' Jazz says eventually, about her smoking.

'That's what my husband says,' comments Aruna. 'It may be disgusting, but it's necessary. It calms me down. You remember what I got like.'

'Too well,' says Jazz, and he finally pulls out the paper packet and throws it over to Aruna, who catches it on her lap.

'What's that?' she starts to say, but he sees her stop herself when she recognizes the name of the pharmacy, and the familiar green and yellow logo on the bag. When she recognizes the bag itself. It was the last set of meds that Jazz had picked up for her, the morning before they had gone to the clinic for their test results.

'Two years old, but I'm guessing they haven't expired, and they're better than nothing. Better than drinking yourself to oblivion and smoking like a chimney. Besides, we're in Malaysia now, they don't approve of good Muslim women dropping down drunk over the border.'

'I'm not taking them,' says Aruna, casually flinging them back to Jazz.

'Fine,' he says. 'Then I'm not taking you to see my dad.' Aruna looks at him, and his mouth is a hard, firm line; it is the sort of expression she imagines a disapproving mother would give an errant teenager.

'I don't need you, I've already arranged to see him,' she says matter-of-factly.

'I know, but you called the nurse from the speed dial on my phone. You haven't a clue where he is, and you haven't got a number to find out. I hope you have a fun few days in KL looking for him, Hassan's a very common name.'

Aruna looks at him crossly, outmanoeuvred, and grabs back the packet, taking her pills and downing them with a swig of cola. In fact, she doesn't need to drink anything to swallow the pills, but she doesn't want Jazz to see her swallowing them dry, a talent she has left from her previous junkie days.

'You mean Ahsan,' she says eventually. 'Your name's Ahsan, or did you forget?'

'My dad's always gone by his middle name, Hassan, has done for years. He never uses Ahsan, except on official documents like his passport. Something to do with there being another writer in the forties with a similar name, I think.'

Aruna can't believe she's been so stupid. 'You mean that your dad's Hari Hassan?' She pulls out the book that Jazz had given her. 'This is his collected works? Why didn't you tell me? I mean, you never talked about your dad's writing, I just assumed he'd always been a journalist.' She looks at what Jazz had written, 'For my dearest Rooney, Always and Forever Yours, Jazz,' dated the month before she left.

Jazz looks embarrassed, 'I guess I wanted to know your professional opinion on his work. To see if he really was as good as everyone said he was, as he thought he was. It was so annoying that you never gave it a second glance, it just sat there on your desk in the apartment.'

'It just seemed a bit irrelevant,' admits Aruna, 'the collected works of a minor, well-reputed poet who I'd never expressed an interest in or studied.' She runs a finger along the spine thoughtfully, 'I took it with me, though,' she says. 'I guess I just wanted something from home; it was the last thing you gave me.'

'The last thing you gave me was a broken heart,' says Jazz, and then laughs in self-mockery. 'God, I've waited two years to say that, and when I do it sounds like a line from a trashy book. You know the sort. One of mine.'

He looks out of the window, tapping his fingers, 'We never gave each other much, did we?'

'We always said it would have been like giving something to ourselves,' replies Aruna. 'And you know what, we were right.'

'Nice to know we were right about something, Rooney,' says Jazz. He is becoming a little disappointed with himself at how easy it is to reminisce, as though they are an old divorced couple catching up over a bridge hand. He wants to feel an edge, to feel passion and fury; he wants to be a physical threat, and drag her into an embrace. 'You said that there was something in the book that brought you back,' he says. 'What was it?'

'You'll think it doesn't make sense. It was something completely random, really. I was looking at the book over breakfast, after Patrick had left for work. I told myself it was because it would be useful for my research, but the truth is, we'd quarrelled, and I just wanted to touch something to do with my old life. And then there was this line that leapt out at me. And then I left. And I came back home.'

'Just like that,' says Jazz, looking unconvinced.

'Just like that,' says Aruna, 'Or near as. I got dressed first. But not washed.' She flicks through the book, and finds the letter from 1971. 'Here it is,' she says, and he sits beside her to read it, pushing away the cola bottle and pungent remains of masala dosa and fried fish.

'My brother enemy,' he says out loud. 'There will

always be a place for you in my heart but there is no longer a place for you in my country . . .' He reads the rest, and looks up, realizing how close he is to Aruna, her thigh jammed against his on the narrow seat, her lip trembling a touch, until she bites it still. There is a bead of perspiration on her forehead, just under her hairline, and he can smell the shampoo in her hair through the other thicker, greasier scents of the train.

'My brother enemy,' she repeats softly, as she reaches over and closes the book, as though asking him something. In reply Jazz pulls her roughly into his arms after all, and kisses her for the first time since their separation, with passion, with fury, with untempered violence; and within a moment she responds just as viciously, kissing him back, with biting teeth and digging nails. It is a collision of flesh and bones rather than an embrace, with no more tenderness or sense than a car crash, as they taste the blood on swollen lips, take each other's air with heavy, laboured breaths, and score flesh with bruising grips. Then, just as quickly, they both stop, and become limp as the red, angry heat leaks from them, leaving them wrung out like damp cloths. Aruna pushes him easily away, and he collapses back into his seat opposite her, burying his head in his hands, his back curved over in defeat, while she leans ashen-faced against the frame of the window. Jazz feels as though he's been in a physical fight, as though he's been punched several times over in the gut; he has the iron taste of blood in his mouth, either his or hers, and swallows it down. Aruna looks sick, disgusted with herself; she doesn't glance back at him, and pulling out another cigarette she continues to smoke.

'Twenty years, Rooney,' Jazz finally says bitterly. 'We've known each other for over twenty years. I loved you when you still wore pigtails and braces. I waited for you while you were away in college, I looked after you when your dad died, I got you your meds, I made sure you ate. You owe me. You owe me more than just sauntering back into my life, and saying that we were over the moment you sauntered out.'

'I know I owe you,' says Aruna. 'I owe you our life back, I owe you children and marriage and a future. But I can't give you what I owe. You're not available to me any more. And because I can't give it to you, I can't give it to anyone.' And with this simple admission, Jazz realizes something. He realizes that Aruna has never stopped loving him, and that she has carried part of him inside her, as fully as her womb carried the physical memory of their three dead children, poor unformed lumps that never even developed lungs to take a first breath. He realizes that he has carried her too, like a body inside him, and that he loved her just as much in her absence as he had when she was in his bed, night after night, when they made perfunctory love that eventually became satisfactory, but was never more than that because it always felt that little bit strange, and because that wasn't what had mattered to them. He knows that he will never again possess and be possessed by someone the way that he has with Aruna. It is as though they were two halves of the same sun that had fallen apart, spinning around in space, with a magnetic connection deep in their cores that meant they were seeking, always seeking the other.

'If we'd never have found out . . .' Jazz starts to ask.

Aruna nods, and interrupts him before he can finish this obvious, painful question. 'You know we would have – stayed together, I mean. Always and Forever Yours, Jazz, you remember?'

'It would have been easier if one of us had just died, like our kids did,' says Jazz at last. 'Just dropped down dead. That would have been closure, wouldn't it? For the one who went at least.'

Aruna glances back at him, with a half-smile around her lips, and a shiny glint in her eyes that might be tears or the hint of her suppressed disorder. 'Jazz,' she says, 'don't you think I thought of that? Don't you think I tried?'

In the months after Aruna's departure and his mother's suspicious death, Jazz was haunted by ghosts. He had suddenly lost the two people aroound whom he had built his life; and yet he saw them everywhere. He saw his mother picking out a cardigan at a mall on Orchard Road, or stepping off the bus at the Botanic Gardens, he saw Aruna's slight form disappearing into a Chinatown cafe, or turning a corner on Raffles Place. He pursued these ghosts to the point of obsession, he believed in magic, he believed in miracles. And when he caught up with the perfectly ordinary middle-aged matrons or young women he had followed, tapping them unapologetically on the shoulder if he got that close, he scowled at them without sympathy for not being the miracle he sought, as though they had tricked him instead of his own helpless mind. He was finally able to understand what Aruna had felt after her own father's death, as he went a little crazy too in his grief, bereaved twice, but with only one body to bury. And he didn't just see Aruna in the other twenty-something Singaporean women she might have superficially resembled, he saw her everywhere; in the paving stones, in the waves of the sea, in reflections in glass, in the shadows of the trees. He saw her everywhere she had once moved, which was the whole island state; his desolation shrouded the city like a smog.

Jazz had cut off all ties to his father after his mother's death; he did not attempt to seek consolation from him, or explanation of the baffling mystery of his and Aruna's shared blood. The mystery itself didn't occupy Jazz, as he was completely occupied by Aruna's absence, the sudden absence that was as loud and incomprehensible as a thunderstorm in a room, and the hope of her eventual return. She had left him no way to contact her, she had left no note for him, no clue to where she might have gone; their friends didn't know what had happened to her either. Jazz contacted the hospitals and the police, and after enduring humiliating interviews in his home, during which the authorities confirmed she probably hadn't been murdered by him and stuffed in the cavity wall, they discovered that she had left Singapore and closed enquiries, pointing out kindly, rather obviously, 'She's just left you, sir. That's all.' As though this was the most reassuring possibility.

In the months that followed his grief became anger. He drank himself into a stupor, and found himself waking up in strange women's beds. He used sex as a weapon to hurt Aruna, rather than to seek a moment of comfort for himself, betraying her the only way he had left. When he let himself back into the home they had shared, stinking with self-pity, stale with sweat and exhausted with dirty passion, he sometimes wondered if she was doing the same. In his clearer moments, he pulled himself together enough to visit his mother's grave, and asked her the obvious questions. Was Aruna his sister? Had his father slept with Aruna's mother? It seemed so unlikely, his father would have been all of thirty years older than her; and she had been in Singapore in the early seventies when Aruna was born, whereas his father had been closeted in Bangladesh with his pregnant mother, supporting the independence movement. So had his mother slept with Aruna's dour father? Jazz couldn't imagine it; they had met each other at school functions, and his mother had liked Aruna, but had rarely commented on her father, except to say the usual platitudes of how 'tragic' his story was, with the untimely death of his young wife and second child. So perhaps Aruna and he had both been secretly kidnapped or bought as babies from some washerwomen in the Bengal, wife and mistress of the same village man who couldn't support any more mouths to feed, and separately sold to their desperate, childless parents? He preferred this last explanation, as it absolved his mother from culpability; she would have had no reason to know about Aruna. He decided that the details of how it had come about didn't really matter, without Aruna there was no reason to know. She hadn't even cared enough to talk to him about it, to explore these possibilities; she had dumped their relationship like a stinking corpse into the sea and sailed away; she had never let him know if she was alive or dead. Perhaps he really was chasing a ghost; perhaps he was more of a ghost himself than he realized.

Jazz began to wonder, through his loneliness, and emptiness, whether suicide was as painless as it seemed. His mother's suicide or murder, if it was that, had been dramatic; she had made her family home a blazing testament to the inutility of her life. Perhaps it was a solution; it seemed so easy, to jump off a boat into the sparkling sea, and just not get back on again, to sink into the amniotic embrace of the water, cushioned by the kindness of the warmth and the wet, like an unborn child before the fluid drains and it is expelled into the sticky air. I can't do it, he mused sadly to himself, I can't do it, because somewhere Aruna might still be in the world. She might have found a way to be happy, or else be barely living like him, getting up in the morning, and going to bed at night, and unsure how to fill the endless hours in between. He couldn't shrug off his life, because Aruna might still be clinging to hers, and he had to be there for her when she came back.

Life, after all, went on. Jazz began to work again, and his writing took on a dark, melancholic edge, his heroes drank to excess and used sex as a weapon, they carried the scent of betrayal about them, and he had his greatest commercial success. He began to meet girls while both he and they were sober, and eventually began to date. He changed around his apartment and replaced some of his furniture, especially the bed, so he could sleep without the memory of Aruna imprinted beside him, so he could walk into the flat and not have that tingle of expectation that she might be home, after all, reading the *Straits Times* with her slippers dangling from her feet, or eating a takeaway, and that he'd just been caught in a long and arduous dream. But he never forgot, and he never stopped waiting. And he knew exactly what he would say when she finally got in touch. He would dismiss the time they had been separated with a magic wand, with pure willpower; he would behave as though she had left the day before, and not months and years before, he would say: 'Where are you, Rooney? I'll come and get you.'

'I never tried,' replies Jazz. 'I was waiting for you. I wanted to be here for you if you needed me. When you needed me. I knew you'd come back; I believed it, so it had to happen.' He is holding her hand again, and neither of them is quite sure how it came about, they do not know who reached out to whom.

'Like magic,' says Aruna ruefully. 'Part of me never left, I guess.'

'Do you think you'd have even thought about ending it, if you'd been on your medication?' asks Jazz.

'Maybe not,' says Aruna. 'I just needed to escape. Everything. It seemed such a simple way out. Just having a swim, and not coming back.'

'Why didn't you go through with it?' asks Jazz.

'I don't know. It wasn't as easy as it seemed. I felt guilty, for you, for Patrick. The guilt wasn't enough to weigh me down. It just made me float, like I was full of too much air.' She laughs bitterly, 'Maybe I didn't go through with it, so you could have the pleasure of doing it for me. Just taking my heart, and skewering it dripping on a knife, like the brother in *'Tis Pity*.'

'I don't have to take something I've always had,' says Jazz. As he makes this outrageous claim, he realizes that it is true. Holding Aruna's hand for his own comfort, feeling the slight stickiness of their palms, the way that their fingers wrap around their knuckles in a lock snug enough to swing by, he wonders if he will ever be able to give back what he no longer has the right to own.

Aruna

Ekspres Sinaran Train, Singapore to Kuala Lumpur

Aruna didn't realize that she had fallen asleep, but she must have, as she finds herself waking, and leaning lightly against Jazz, who had probably moved beside her to support her. He is asleep himself, and she allows herself the luxury of staring at his face; he was always a graceful sleeper, his mouth is firm, and his face has the calmness and warmth of terracotta. They have the same mouth, the same eyes, but it sometimes felt that they shared more than that, the same flesh, the same blood, more literally than they realized; he had never needed to be inside her to feel like part of her, as though the separation of their skin was just something superficial, as though they really were parts of the same body, waves in the same heaving sea. She closes her eyes, and listens to him breathing, marvelling at the ease of this intimacy; in the increasingly crowded, raucous train carriage, it feels as though they are alone together in a room, and that nothing else exists beyond the ribbons of breath between them.

184

Her phone beeps softly, a little plaintive cry that it has when it is running low on battery, and she pulls it out of her handbag in time to see the photo of Patrick and herself on their wedding day dissolve and disappear with a wink, as the phone switches itself off. Patrick will be waking up himself now, it is early morning in London, and she thinks about everything that she doesn't know about him, that she has never let herself know. She knows the colour of his hair and eyes, of course, but she doesn't know his exact height, she has no idea of his weight, she isn't sure if he was thirty-four or thirty-five when they first met, and she knows that his birthday is in early August, but not precisely when. Everything that she had tacitly accused him of when she left, she is equally guilty of. And she realizes that she has never, in their eighteen months together, in their year of marriage, watched him sleep.

Aruna groaned under her duvet as the light filtered through their curtains, and opened her eyes cautiously to find Patrick already awake and looking at her. He was unembarrassed to be caught out; he always seemed to be looking at her with an implicit question, as though she were a book that might be read. She wondered if her unconscious body gave away more than she realized, if she breathed out demons and secrets while she slept. 'I really wish you'd stop doing that,' she muttered.

'What?'

'Looking at me when I'm asleep. Or trying to sleep. It's creepy.'

'It's the only time I can look at you properly,' he said. 'When you're awake you've always got your face in a book, or your laptop, or scoffing a Chinese takeaway.' He went to kiss her cheek, and almost got her ear instead, as she had already turned away from him crossly. 'And at least you're not in a mood when you sleep,' he commented. 'Sometimes it's a lot more fun looking at you than listening to you.'

'I could say the same,' muttered Aruna into her pillow.

'I'm not sure you do either, that often,' said Patrick. He put his arms suddenly around her with impetuous affection, pressing his long, hard torso against her, and gently kissed her neck, just above her collarbone where her blood pulsed, his lips placed with a precision that artlessly showed his detailed knowledge of her body's map. Aruna breathed out an instinctive moan before she even realized it, but then Patrick got up, just as suddenly, and left the room. 'Coffee?' he called out from the corridor.

'Great,' she replied listlessly. She pulled on an enormous fleece dressing gown that drowned her; she still hadn't got used to the British winter, she had no idea how West End girls could flit between taxis and nightclubs with bare legs and strappy tops in the icy early hours, and how Patrick could walk naked to the kitchen and not even feel the cold. She followed him, and sat down on the pine kitchen floorboards with her back against the radiator, her legs splayed out with the louche carelessness of an adolescent. Patrick put her coffee on the counter, and as she showed no sign of shifting from the only heat source in the room, picked it up and handed it to her. She remained on the floor, wrapped in her dressing-gown blanket, and pressed the warm mug to her cheek.

'You know, it's not that cold,' said Patrick, going back towards the bathroom to shower.

'No, it's not cold. It's fucking freezing,' she complained. 'The heating in these Victorian buildings is ridiculous.' She never understood why the British seemed so keen on old houses, with high ceilings and gaps under the doors and mouldy original sash windows with single panes of floated glass, that meant they never heated up. She preferred modern homes with insulation and double glazing, homes which didn't have seasons but could remain in a balmy early summer all year round. Her coffee cooled, and she left it half drunk, and then went back to bed.

'Bathroom's free,' said Patrick cheerfully. 'We've got to go in an hour, or we'll be late.'

'I'm not sure I can be bothered to trek all the way to the back of bloody beyond to see your family,' said Aruna carelessly. 'I might give it a miss.'

'You can't,' he said flatly. 'You didn't turn up the last

time. Or the time before that. And this is our Christmas get-together. Seeing as you've refused to spend the actual day with them.'

'Because we did Christmas with them last year,' said Aruna, 'You inflicted them on me for two whole days, when we'd only just started living together. And you know, you needn't be so intolerant. Christmas just isn't that big a deal where I'm from. Why don't we see them on Chinese New Year instead?' she added flippantly. She wondered why she was being so difficult, and then she realized the reasons, hoping that Patrick hadn't guessed. She was punishing him for looking at her while she slept, when he knew she could put no barriers up; she was punishing him for not bothering to make love to her that morning. She was possibly even punishing him for having a family which he cared about, when she, in a world and at a season awash with families, was singularly alone. 'And your mum loathes me, anyway,' she muttered.

'She doesn't loathe you,' he replied patiently, 'but you could try a bit more with her. You're always so cold and distant.' His accusation was perfectly justified; Aruna was cold, because it was always cold in this stupid country, and she was distant, because part of her was still a long way away. And she found it hard enough to be warm and close to her own husband, much less to the strangers to whom he had once belonged.

'Charming. Now I'm definitely not going,' said Aruna.

'Well, I'm not going without you,' said Patrick, 'so you're coming if I have to tie you up and bundle you in the boot. You know I could do it,' he added, with a voice that was half-threatening and half-joking, 'I could pick you up with one hand if I wanted.'

Aruna simply scoffed, and rolled over. But Patrick refused to be dismissed, and slid back under the duvet with her, his shower-fresh body as damp and warm as the breeze over the South China Sea. Aruna felt a sudden pang of nostalgia deep in her gut that she associated with thoughts of home, and an uneasy confusion that Patrick's flesh against hers should be what had evoked the memory. 'Please come,' he said, his breath against her ear, sliding his large, capable hands up her stomach, over her breasts, and then generously back down again. So Aruna did after all; as she went for lunch with her in-laws, she was unable to decide which of them had manipulated, and which of them had capitulated, the more.

Lunch was at Patrick's parents' house in Kent, and they bickered all the way around the M25, before lapsing into sullen silence. When they arrived, shortly after Patrick's younger brother and brood of three, Aruna made determined small talk with the interest that she normally reserved for strangers, whom she found were less likely to bore or disappoint. She talked about the weather, asked after health and holiday plans, enquired about work, insincerely admired clothing, new haircuts and offspring and used a plethora of mild English platitudes in subtle mockery, 'Oh my, how lovely,' 'How perfectly delicious,' 'How very clever of you,' 'So you must be delighted,' 'Well, thank you, how kind.' She expected Patrick would be annoyed at her again for being so obviously phoney, but instead he beamed at her with pride when he caught her eye. When she helpfully took the plates into the kitchen, he followed her, and caught her in his arms. 'Thank you for making so much effort today,' he said. 'I love you for trying.' And he kissed her with such grateful tenderness, that Aruna knew what he was really thinking but hadn't wanted to raise her defences by saying out loud; he thought, at that moment, not just that he loved her, but that she loved him; he thought that making an effort with his dull family was her way of showing that she loved him. He always saw her as someone better than who she really was, but yet again Aruna found that she liked being mistaken for this person, who was kind rather than hypocritical, who was motivated by love rather than self-interest or bloody-mindedness. And so she kissed him back.

'Oops, sorry,' said Patrick's brother, Graham, as he backed into the kitchen with more dishes. 'If you're going to snog like teenagers, do it somewhere more private.' Patrick laughed, and with his arm protectively around Aruna, pulled her out to the hallway. 'Wait until you have kids,' Graham called after them a bit peevishly. 'Then you'll kiss on the first of the month and cuddle on match days.' Aruna glanced back at the note of discontent in his voice, and caught him giving her a long

190

brooding look mixed with discomfort, which might have been caused by over-eating, but which seemed sus- piciously like misplaced lust.

Back in the living room, plump with overripe floral sofas and armchairs in puffy leather, Graham's wife Cerys was breastfeeding their latest addition, a petulant pink and white baby girl with a fluff of blonde hair and round edible cheeks, like sugar treats. Aruna tried not to look at the veined, pale breast with the rosy-nosed sore-looking nipple that the cross infant kept spitting out; she felt a cramp in her own stomach that was nothing to do with over-eating. 'Oh hell! Sorry, pardon my language, Ar-oon- ah,' said Cerys, who made a habit of over-pronouncing her name which Aruna found profoundly irritating; she often had to resist returning the favour, and lilting back Ce-ry-ees with swollen Welsh vowels. 'Melanie's just not having it today.'

'Maybe she's just had enough,' said Aruna, who knew how the baby felt. Her diagnosis was instantly confirmed by Melanie vomiting over her mother, which she com- bined with a burp and an over-satisfied smile. Aruna sup- pressed the urge to smile back complicitly, as Cerys gave her a resentful glance for daring to have been right. 'Oh, how ghastly, you poor thing,' she said to Cerys, uncon- sciously aping her mother-in-law, who instead of being annoyed, nodded with apparent approval at Aruna for using this snippet of shared vocabulary. Aruna realized then that her mother-in-law was playing the phoney too. She was struck by the ridiculousness of this family meal, where real feelings were hidden beneath a flaky veneer of politeness, which fooled nobody at all; it was like they were all animated puppets on a stage, Patrick was the only one with the sincerity to play himself.

'Would you mind?' said Cerys, dumping the baby on Aruna before she could say whether she did, and dabbing at the baby-sick with the muslin draped over her shoulder. Aruna held Melanie gingerly at arm's length, but as this seemed awkward for both of them, she slowly brought her closer, as though the child's milky warmth could alleviate the cramp in her abdomen, the hollow sense of longing for what had been lost. She eventually held the baby against her flat bosom, and Melanie nestled there comfortably, shifting her nappied bottom into the crook of her arm and giving a contented yawn.

'She likes you,' said Cerys almost crossly, looking at her daughter as though she was somehow being disloyal.

Patrick, who'd been caught in a long conversation with his dad about his various trivial ailments, walked across to Aruna as soon as he saw her holding his niece. He smiled at the stunned bewilderment in her face as the baby settled against her, and said carelessly, 'So, are you coming round to getting one of these?'

'Sorry, I need the loo,' said Aruna suddenly, and handing the child unceremoniously back to Cerys, all but ran upstairs, where she retched dryly and silently into the toilet bowl. She then closed the seat and sat back, letting tears run down her face.

As Aruna quietly left the bathroom, conscious of the inappropriate amount of time she'd spent there, she heard her mother-in-law talking to Graham in the downstairs corridor. 'I still don't see why Pat couldn't have got himself a *nice* girl,' her mother-in-law said, 'I mean, he's a doctor. And just look at him, he's a catch.'

'Do you mean a nice white girl?' asked Graham, clearly unsure if his mother was being unacceptably prejudiced.

'No, I don't mean that,' she said impatiently to her son at his accusation. 'I just meant a nice girl. And she's not. I know that she's all very clever and so on, with her degrees and her Mandarin, but she just seems a bit . . .'

'What?' asked Graham.

'Well, sluttish, darling,' said his mother at last. 'I mean, the way she looks at him sometimes, it's so blatant, like a cat looking at a mouse – like he's dinner. And Pat's always touching her, always. Her neck, her arm, her waist, her knee. Stroking her even, in public, it's so in-appropriate.'

'They were French kissing in the kitchen, just now,' agreed Graham. 'Maybe they're just in love.'

'He's just obsessed with her, more like. It's as though she's some kind of sexual predator who's trapped him. And she hardly ever smiles at Pat, did you notice that? I'm not sure she even likes him. I think she's just using him, and when she's had enough, she'll just leave him and move on. My poor little boy.'

'I'd stop worrying, Mum,' said Graham, 'You sound a

little jealous. She must like him a bit, she married him, didn't she? And I know a lot of people who'd wish their wives were a bit less . . . *nice*.'

On the long drive back, Patrick had to take the wheel again; it should have been Aruna's turn, but she had drunk too much, as usual. 'Your mother thinks I'm some kind of eastern whore,' she announced, 'who's holding you in thrall with my whoreish sexual wiles.'

'What gives you that idea?' said Patrick evenly. 'One and a half bottles of Merlot?'

'One and a half minutes of eavesdropping. I heard her say that I was some heartless slut who'd trapped you.'

'That's completely out of order,' he responded in immediate and gratifying outrage. 'I'm sorry you heard that, she's a shitty old bigot, sometimes. I'll talk to her about that and get her to damn well apologize.'

'You're taking my side over your family's?' said Aruna in surprise, 'How do you know I'm not making it up?'

'Well, you're not, are you?' said Patrick, 'And you're my family too, now, whether you believe it or not.' There was a pause while Aruna absorbed this disquieting, surprising fact, and Patrick glanced at her curiously, unable to tell whether his declaration had pleased her. 'Speaking of family, did you say anything to my brother?' he asked eventually. 'I mean, did you flirt with him, or something?'

'Oh, God no,' said Aruna, who didn't find Graham in

the slightest bit attractive; Patrick was clearly the victor in his family, with a stature and sporty physique and well-scrubbed good looks that surpassed what he might have expected to have inherited from his bland parents. Graham just looked like a younger version of his dad.

'I think he's got a bit of a thing for you. He kept staring at you when you weren't looking, and he made a really inappropriate comment about you, which I'm not going to dignify by repeating.'

'He's just not getting any at home at the moment,' said Aruna dismissively. 'It's no big deal – he's probably doing the same thing to the secretaries at work.'

'Still, I don't think we'll see them for a while,' said Patrick decisively, 'until he's got over his crush. I'm not having my little brother drooling over my wife, and I don't want you to have to feel awkward around him.' He carried on driving, and then said casually, 'Still, little Melanie's a delight, isn't she?'

'Adorable,' said Aruna cautiously.

'You know, we've been married for over nine months now. I know what you said back in the summer, but I really think we should start trying for some kids of our own,' he said, still too casually. Patrick tended to drive one-handed, with the other resting on her lap or holding her own hand, letting go just long enough to change gear; his mother was right, he was always touching her, but Aruna had never minded it; she had simply accepted his touch, his physical affection, as her due. His palm resting over her knee, the brushing of the back of her neck when he stood behind her, the absent-minded stroking of the bare flesh of her upper arms from her sleeves to her elbow, his arm pressing warmly around the curve of her waist; as though reassuring himself with his constant touch that she was real, as though reassuring her as well. Aruna noticed how his right hand, normally spread and relaxed on the wheel, was gripping it tightly enough for his knuckles to bulge in shining white detail. She wondered how long he'd been wanting to have this conversation; in the little time they spent together in the evenings, she didn't often give him much opportunity; if he looked like he was going to talk about something awkward, she could always find an excuse to leave the room, or busy herself at her laptop with an apologetic, 'Do you mind? I really need to get this done.' The one place she couldn't escape was on a long car journey. She realized that he had already planned this discussion in the morning, which was why he was so insistent on her coming; he wanted her alone in the car, to ask her to have his babies, the latest in his string of demands, the only one she had so far refused: Stay for Breakfast, Stay Forever, Marry Me, Have My Child. She wondered whether taking her side against his awful mother and potentially lecherous brother might have been an equally calculated move; as though he expected her to repay his loyalty with pregnancies. 'I'd really like to,' he said when she didn't reply, 'in case you hadn't worked that out.'

'I don't think so,' said Aruna flatly. 'I haven't changed my mind.'

'You'd be a great mother,' continued Patrick, as though she hadn't spoken. 'Did you see how little Melanie calmed down in a moment with you? You're a natural.'

'I said no,' said Aruna, 'I don't want to start trying for kids.' She paused, and said, 'Sorry.'

'You can't just say sorry and think that'll be the end of it,' said Patrick. 'Why the hell not? No one's getting any younger here, you know.' And a long argument on this persistent subject began. That night Patrick slept on the sofa, and Aruna slept fitfully in their bed, which felt absurdly too big without him in it, but thought with mixed-up relief that at least no one would be watching her breathing out her private demons while she slept.

Jazz stirs and, opening his eyes, looks straight into Aruna's. 'Sorry,' he says, 'I didn't realize I'd nodded off. I only meant to shut my eyes.'

'Do you think that I'd have made a good mother?' she asks him.

He nods, and if he is surprised at the question he doesn't show it. 'Of course you would. The best.' Aruna gives a small uncertain smile; she is uncomfortably aware that she has so far not been a good daughter, a good wife or even a good friend. And so she is unsure that she merits his confidence in this matter.

Hassan

Kuala Lumpur General Hospital, Malaysia

Alone in his room, Hari Hassan is reading the other letters between himself and Anwar from the early seventies. 'Our friendship,' Anwar wrote in a letter following Hassan's marriage, 'is a soul shared between two bodies.' He was paraphrasing Aristotle, although he didn't mention it; perhaps he assumed Hassan would already know. And yet it was during this time that their friendship was most strongly tested. Anwar's cousin, Ali Bhutto, had become an important man on the national stage with high political ambition; with his family connections, Anwar soon found himself an influential figure in the West Pakistani army. He had seemed initially pleased with his success, perhaps even a little bit smug, but that was during peacetime, with occasional border skirmishes to handle. Neither he nor Hassan conceived of anything as horrific as the civil war that would erupt when East Pakistan declared itself independent as Bangladesh. The West Pakistani army was swift and vicious in response, thousands were reputedly killed in the fighting, and more disquieting rumours were being circulated, of women raped by soldiers with such cold-blooded consistency and thoroughness, it was as though they were trying to cleanse the ethnicity of the next generation of Bengalis, of children slaughtered as casually as animals. Anwar heard of the atrocities third-hand, in the relative comfort of the senior ranks; having congratulated himself so fulsomely for saving one woman and child, he now found himself with the blood of multitudes on his hands. 'I have the choice of betraying my country, or betraying all that I hold good,' he wrote plaintively. 'I don't have the strength to betray my country, and so I am betraying my integrity, and my friends. I will always be your brother, but now I am your enemy.'

Hassan wrote a reply, but he never heard a response from Anwar, and never knew if he had received it. And so he recklessly published his letter instead in the national newspapers; this is the letter that Hassan finds now, the fragile cutting falling out of the diary, the paper and ink as faded as that of a pressed flower. 'My brother enemy, have the guts to leave this job unfinished, to do all in your power to cease this terrible conflict that sets brother against brother. Have the guts to betray your pride rather than your friends. Let our actions before God, and not our actions in war, be those by which we are judged,' he reads from fine newsprint with difficulty, half remembering as well as reading. 'My brother enemy,' his letter finally closes, 'the green and pleasant land is red with the

blood of brave men, broken women and innocent children, and the calls for vengeance will not and should not
be silenced. My brother, my enemy. It's time to stop
fighting, and go home.' He had not mentioned Anwar's
name in the letter; those who read it assumed that the
brother enemy was the state of Pakistan; as before, his
private writings had been given a public significance. At
the time it was published, only Anwar would have known
that the letter was for him. Ironically, this letter would
turn out to be Hari Hassan's most famous piece of work.
Hassan folds the article up, and slips it back in the
leather-bound diary with the other letters.

Khalid Shah arrives in the early evening, and is far from
his usual bluff self. He blunders in nervously, and fails to
look Hassan in the eye, as though he is a junior doctor
who has been forced to give bad news, and has no idea
where to start. 'What's wrong?' says Hassan, feeling a
guilty thrill to be able to ask this of someone else for
a change, no matter how distressed Khalid appeared.
Hassan supposes that he should relish this moment, as at
his stage of dying, opportunities for future guilty thrills
are limited.

'Chief, I read the last of Abbu's diaries today,' said
Khalid, looking at him meaningfully.

Hassan looks blankly at him, aware that Khalid is
awaiting some kind of specific response, and has no idea

what would be appropriate. 'Well done,' he says eventually. 'They must have taken you an age to go through. You must be pleased to have completed them.'

Khalid looks at him sadly, 'You really don't know, do you? I didn't think you did. There was a letter to you there, but it was an original, not a copy. I'd guessed he'd never sent it.'

'Another letter?' asks Hassan, wondering why he is meant to be overawed by this news; he has hundreds of letters from Anwar. He feels a slight anxiety already descending that he has to read another one.

'Here, Chief,' says Khalid, unfolding it and passing it to him. 'I don't know how to say any of it, so it's better you hear it from Abbu.' He is obviously not intending to wait while Hassan reads the letter, and hastily takes his leave. 'I'm sorry,' he says briefly, turning back at the door. 'I'm so sorry for it all.' He has only been gone for a few seconds, when he returns with a timing that is almost inappropriately funny, 'Needless to say, I won't pursue the publication of the diaries, Chief.'

Hassan looks at the letter calmly, wondering what the fuss is about. He traces his hand across the page, still crisp and clean although it was dated a couple of years back, with the pale blue paper that Anwar had always favoured.

'My dear Hari,' he reads, in Anwar's familiar hand,

grown a little more careless and scratchy with age: 'I have always thought of you as my closest friend, and as my true brother, truer than those who share my blood. And I confess to you now that I have always been jealous of you, and what you have achieved. I feel I have always been one step behind you, and trying to step out of your shadow; you were my mentor at Oxford, my protector during the War, you sponsored my writing career. We all knew that I was not as clever, as brave, or as inspired as you. My best writing was not original, and my original writing was not my best, and you will recognize that I have borrowed even that line from our much-admired Samuel Johnson. The only thing in which I excelled was my army career, and that, eventually, filled me with shame. I have always considered my greatest deed, aside from marrying the best of wives and fathering my children, was in sending Zaida to you, and saving both her and little Jazz from a terrible fate.

And so we come to my true confession, for that is what this is. I have only you and God to judge me, and I suspect that God will not be kind. You will know that Zaida was exceedingly generous to me when Meeru passed away; you will not know that her generosity led to my affection, and once more one step behind you, we began a relationship of a more intimate nature. When Zaida's cancer was diagnosed, I suspect that I was more distressed than you. She did not wish to live in the shadow of the disease. She lied to you and Jazz when she said she was in remission, and she asked me to help her end her life. And because I loved her, I agreed. She took her life with pills I had procured the morning you went to Melaka, and I did as I promised, and set fire to your kitchen to make it appear an accident. I did not expect the fire to spread so extensively. I killed your wife, Hari, and as I am finding it hard to live with the guilt and to live without her, and because I am an old and foolish man, I will follow her path. I have no need to set my own kitchen on fire, as there is nothing very suspicious about someone of my age suddenly passing. I'm sorry, Hari, I'm so sorry for it all.'

Hassan looks closely at the bottom of the letter, but there is no signature. Anwar had not decided the letter was over, he perhaps had felt that there was something more to say. Hassan feels no anger at his old friend; he feels relief, a fluid feeling that flushes through his sagging, useless flesh, that he was not responsible for Zaida's death, after all. He feels relief that, at the end of her life, she found love. He hopes that God chose his own, and was kind to his friend. The only sense of regret he has is for the missing words that Anwar never wrote, the message from the dead that he will never hear.

Jazz

Kuala Lumpur General Hospital, Malaysia

Jazz and Aruna enter the hospital shortly after Khalid Shah leaves; Jazz recognizes the avuncular figure making his way through the car park, and hangs back to avoid having to talk to him. 'Who's that?' asks Aruna in amusement.

'Just Baba's friend's son, Khalid,' says Jazz. 'He's possibly the most boring man in KL.'

Aruna goes to the office, and asks about seeing Hari Hassan, and Jazz can't stop himself smiling when he hears her speak. It feels good to smile, to be someone who feels humour rather than pathos between them; he enjoys the smile so much that he practically allows himself to grin. 'What's so funny?' Aruna asks, in an annoyed tone.

'The way you're speaking Bahasa with that clipped oh-so-lovely-scones-and-tea English accent. It's hilarious. It's even thicker than it was when you came back from college.'

Aruna looks at him, and smiles back indulgently while she waits for the administrator to fill in some paperwork. 'Speaking of college, what did you mean, in the coffee shop, when you said that we had things to fight about after college? What was there to fight about?'

'You know what,' says Jazz, 'We just never talked about it.'

'Oh.' Aruna realizes. 'Of course. That.'

'It was just so obvious, the moment we first got together once you were back, that you'd slept with other people.'

'I did it for us, in a way,' says Aruna. 'I wanted to know that I wasn't frigid.' She pauses and says, 'It was obvious you had too.'

'I wanted to be sure that I really knew what I was doing,' says Jazz, 'but there wasn't any point discussing it, as we both knew anyway. We didn't even fight about infidelity.'

'We were never about that,' says Aruna. Jazz wonders, as she says this, what she thinks that they really were about.

When Jazz was ten years old, his parents moved to Singapore for his father's work, where they were to stay for the next nine years; they went from a rambling house in KL with an overgrown garden, to a humid but modern apartment, with a small patio. He had left all his friends, and although he could speak English and Bahasa, he felt that his accent was somehow wrong, and that no one understood him; he was a foreigner in an unfriendly country, where everything moved too fast, where there were too many inexplicable rules, and where children were swatted aside like flies. Just a couple of weeks after their arrival, Jazz started at an English-speaking international school, and went through the motions of the school day without feeling it was anything to do with him, just waiting until he could return to the strange apartment for the comforting smell of his mother's cooking, and bask in her delight, fresh-baked and warm every day like new bread, at seeing him come home. Jazz sat at the back of the class, and noticed that at the front was a girl with two long plaits and braces, who looked vaguely familiar. He wanted to ask her if he knew her, but didn't, as that would have been stupid; of course he didn't know her. But sometimes she glanced back at him as though she had the same question. She was given the first coat peg and locker in their cloakroom, as her initials were AA, Aruna Ahmed. His peg was next to hers, Ejaz Ahsan.

One day, an obnoxious, chubby girl called Winnie was being mean to Aruna, pulling her long plaits, possibly with jealousy, because Winnie's own hair had been economically cropped to a bowl-like bob. 'Piggy-piggy pigtails,' taunted Winnie, 'you've got hair like a five year old!' and when Aruna pushed her away, Winnie pushed her back, harder, so that she fell and grazed her knee. 'Oink-oink,' crowed Winnie in triumph, but was pushed away in her turn by Jazz, who had seen what was happening from his usual lonely place on the low wall. He had run over, and instinctively gave Winnie a casual but firm shove in the chest, so that she fell back on her comfortably cushioned rump, and then he took Aruna by the hand to the cloakrooms, to wash her bleeding knee. It was when they were there, propping her knee up to the long white sink, that he looked at their faces side by side in the mirror and realized what had been so familiar about her; she looked just like him.

'Thanks, Ejaz,' said Aruna. 'Winnie's just such a moron.'

'Yeah, she's a Pooh!' he replied. 'Geddit? Winnie-the-Pooh?'

Aruna nodded, grinning with the slightly goofy expression she had before her braces finally came off. She looked back at the mirror, and pulled at her plaits. 'I hate these. It's the only way Betty knows how to do my hair.'

'Who's Betty? Your sister?' asked Jazz.

'No, I don't have any sisters. Betty's the housekeeper, but she looks after me before and after school, when Dad's working. I haven't got a mum,' said Aruna. She mentioned the last fact mildly, without reproach or sadness, as someone might say that they haven't got a cold, or an umbrella. Jazz couldn't imagine the horror of not having a mum, and his childish heart went out to her yet again.

'You should come back to mine after school one day,'

said Jazz. 'My mum will probably know how to fix your hair in lots of different ways; she's got really long hair.' He said this last fact with pride. He had always been in awe of the beauty of his Amma's hair, and when he was little he used to borrow her combs and clips and sparkly grips, and snag them into his own hair, thinking he might look as pretty as her.

'Sure, that would be cool. I'll check with my dad,' said Aruna. The bell signalling the end of break went, and she said, 'You coming back to class, Ejaz?'

'It's Jazz, not Ejaz,' he said, 'Everyone calls me Jazz. I mean not here, but my friends back home, and my family.'

'My Baba calls me Rooney,' said Aruna, with a shrug. 'It's what my mum called me before she died. It's a baby name, really, I suppose. I was only three when she went.'

'I like Rooney,' said Jazz, 'it suits you.' They went together to class, and later on they sat together for lunch, sharing the snacks they had brought from home. And Jazz, for the first time since he had come to Singapore, didn't feel alone in that strange city. Jazz had appointed himself as Aruna's protector that day without really realizing it, and without being aware that he had already set the tone for their whole future relationship; it was a role he never really gave up.

Jazz looks at Aruna now, and feels that same protective sense he had all those years ago, an urge to protect her that was so deep and invasive it was almost a physical instinct, like the one that had set him running across the playground that day, in the first week of school. Perhaps that was what they had always been about before – he the carer, she the cared-for – but for two years now Aruna has survived without his protection. She had been a stranger in a foreign country, just as he had once been; and she had found employment, friends, a home, a husband. She had mismanaged her own medical treatment, she had drunk and smoked too much, she had considered and retreated from suicide, she had returned with determination to where the bodies of the past were buried; she had made mistakes, but she had also made brave decisions, and she had done it all on her own. He recognizes now that it was always his need to protect, rather than hers; he had played her keeper, but perhaps she had never really needed to be kept. And that if he hadn't been there that first day, Aruna wouldn't have missed his protection at all; perhaps she would have simply got up, dusted herself off, and carried on.

'OK, you can go through now,' says the hospital administrator, passing them both visitors' badges. They go up in the lift, but when they reach the door to Hassan's ward, Aruna turns to see that Jazz has stopped walking.

'Well, are you coming?' she asks.

Jazz shakes his head. 'I think it would be better if it was just you,' he says.

'Because you don't want to see your dad?' she asks. Jazz knows that it seems ridiculous, after having come all this way.

'Not just because of that,' he tries to explain. 'It's because this is all you, Rooney. This is your journey. I'm just going to sit down here and wait for you. I'll watch out for you.' He adds without malice, with a luminous smile, 'It's what I do.' Aruna reaches out for his hand impulsively, and squeezes it, before stepping through the swinging doors.

Aruna

Kuala Lumpur General Hospital, Malaysia

Aruna knocks on the door. 'Mr Ahsan?' she calls, and walks into the room. She nearly steps back in shock at the sight of Jazz's father: his physical deterioration has rendered him almost unrecognizable. His hair and skin have receded and scaled, leaving his once handsome, almost leonine head, as shifty as a lizard's; his colour has changed to something like grey, and the arms and feet that poke out are thin and hollow looking, as easy to crack as kindling. His sheets and tubes seem to be what is holding him together, like a papier-mâché figurine, or a mummy. She is flooded with pity and slight disgust at the sight of such voluptuous decay, and tries hard not to show it on her face. 'Hey there, Mr Ahsan,' she says, just as she used to when she was an awkward teenager, on the rare occasions that she bumped into him at Jazz's place.

'Hello Rooney,' says Hassan, his voice cracked and half-swallowed but with his usual tone of mild irreverence, 'please don't ask me how I am, or tell me that I'm looking well.'

'I'm sorry,' she says briefly, wondering how she could have ever thought that her own troubles were as bad as they could get, when she at least still had physical health. She thinks of Patrick, working in the hospital day after day, surrounded by death and disease as casual colleagues, and suddenly appreciates why he is always so determinedly optimistic, why he always sees the best in people, why he lives in a world where he believes he is loved, even if his own wife never said the words. He has seen how it could end. 'I had no idea you were this bad,' she adds.

'It's worse than you think,' he says. 'They're so good here at compensating for my wrecked bodily processes that it could take months or even years for me to die. My mind is fine, more's the pity. A bright, shiny marble in a bowl of mush,' he indicates his lunch. 'You know, they mash it now. They don't trust me to chew, so they mash it in case I choke; soon they're going to start tubing it straight down. It's like being a baby again; I'm finishing life like I started it, helpless, flat on my back, and pissing in my bed. Your father was lucky to have had a heart attack; I *dream* of heart attacks.' He pauses, and Aruna is aware that she has been staring at him with unflattering fascination, and blinks and looks away. 'Where's Jazz?' he asks hopefully. 'Is he with you?'

Aruna nods. 'He's outside,' she says. She realizes that she is staring at his feet now, instead of his face, his poor,

212

exposed, translucent feet. She moves unthinkingly to the end of the bed, and tucks them in under his blankets.

Hassan looks at her with surprised gratitude. 'You always were such a kind child, Rooney. You haven't seen me for years, and your first concern is whether I'm cold.' He sighs, looking back towards the door, and says, 'Well, at least he came this far. That's something.' He glances back at Aruna, probably taking in for the first time that she doesn't look that peachy either, and asks, 'Was there something you wanted from me, Rooney? It's good of you to visit, but I can't imagine you came all the way from Singapore just for that.'

'I came from London, even,' says Aruna, 'It's where I've been living.'

'London,' sighs Hassan, 'I've not been to London for years. Do you like it there?'

'It's OK,' says Aruna cautiously. 'A bit cold, I suppose.'

Hassan's eyes close briefly, as he allows himself to sink into the past. 'Do you remember the song about a nightingale singing in Berkeley Square, that famous square in Mayfair? I visited London with Jazz and his mum when he was tiny, but when we went to Berkeley Square, there were no nightingales at all; just a car showroom, an advertising agency, an insurance multinational, and a few winebars, scattered around the green. Jazz was so disappointed, "But where all the nite-nite-gales, Baba?" he asked. "Baba, we lost the nite-nite-gales. All the nite-nite-gales gone!"' Hassan chuckles to himself at the memory.

'Nite-nite-gales,' he repeats. 'Like an old fool I promised him we'd find them. You wouldn't believe the trouble it caused me . . .' he trails away ruefully.

'I did have something to ask you,' says Aruna eventually, sitting warily by his side. She wants to touch his hand, but is worried about dislodging his drip, about the hand itself crumbling like a cracker. It seems absurd that she will find out any answers from this poor ghost who has somehow got left behind. The memory of who Hassan was seems somehow stronger and more present than who he has become, as though Jazz sitting outside would see him with much greater clarity in his mind, than she does in this room.

Hassan looks at her, and smiles his lizard smile. 'Of course. What is it?'

But suddenly Aruna has no idea what to say, or where to begin. It no longer seems right to tell him about her and Jazz's relationship, the doctor's revelation, or any part of that. Instead, she takes a deep breath, and simply asks, 'Did you ever have a daughter?'

And Hassan's face falls back in on itself, and his eyes brighten for a misleading moment, before bleary tears fill them. He replies as though he has been waiting all his life to say, 'Yes, I had a daughter, once.'

Aruna, feeling herself begin to tremble, forces herself to ask calmly, 'What happened to her, Mr Ahsan?'

Hassan shakes his head, and chokes out, 'She was adopted. I never saw her. I never knew what happened to her.'

Aruna can't bring herself to ask the final, obvious question: could she have been me? Instead she asks, evasively, 'Would she have been about my age?'

But then Hassan shakes his head, 'No, my dear child. She would have been some twenty years older than you. She would have been in her fifties now, if she lived.'

Aruna sinks back in her chair. So it wasn't to be as simple as that, after all. She isn't sure what else to say, and Hassan recovers himself, and asks, 'Do you know where she is? Is that why you came?'

'I'm sorry, Hari,' she says again, not sure why she suddenly feels close enough to him to call him by his first name. Perhaps because she has thrown him back into an unhappy moment of his past, and opened up a tragedy that has nothing to do with her. She feels responsible, and she wonders how many other secret tragedies are waiting to be exposed in the world, buried inside people who seem perfectly normal, as they go about their daily business, do their chores and stroll home to their families, with their sleeves rolled up ready for dinner. How many tragedies do ordinary people with ordinary cares hide in the deepest recess of memory, or imprinted across their hearts? It feels as though she could take whole cities, London, Singapore, KL, and shake them upside down like snow globes, until parallel cities of past regrets and secret despairs are shaken out of their hiding places and whirl out and around them. And hers are just another snowflake in the dome; perhaps her cares are ordinary, after all.

She thinks of something, and says ruefully, 'You know, my mother would have been in her fifties, if she had lived, too. I could be your honorary granddaughter,' she adds with a smile, suspecting that the joke is inappropriate, but saying it anyway.

'I never knew your mother,' says Hassan. 'She died very young, didn't she? I remember Zaida telling me.'

'Complications with her second pregnancy,' says Aruna briefly, 'They tried to deliver the baby early, but they both died. There was a name for the condition, I think, but I can't quite remember . . .'

'Eclampsia,' says Hassan with a slight sigh. 'It was probably eclampsia.' He looks at Aruna closely, and says wistfully, 'You know, I always thought you and Jazz had the same eyes, because I used to see you side by side all the time, but in fact, when I look at you on your own, when I look inside your eyes instead of around them, it seems that you've got someone else's eyes altogether.' He stares at her as freely as she had stared at him, with the same inappropriate fascination, and says, 'You have really beautiful eyes, you know. Liquid eyes. Swimmable. Drown-innable. I never thought I'd see eyes like that again. How could I never have noticed?' He laughs slightly, almost mocking himself. 'You must think me very fond and foolish, Rooney,' he says, 'but how I wish you really were my granddaughter.'

Aruna reaches for his hand, dismissing her fear of touching death, and his hand under hers doesn't break

216

after all. She passes him her warmth through her palm, through her fingertips. 'I'll take the honorary role,' she says, 'with pleasure. It would be nice to be someone's granddaughter again.' She realizes that if Hassan isn't her father, the only alternative is that he isn't Jazz's either, that Jazz was either fathered by someone else, or adopted. 'I'm sorry to have to ask this, Hari, but I need to know, I must know. Is Jazz really your son, yours and Auntie Zaida's?'

'Of course he's our son,' says Hassan belligerently, but then he realizes from Aruna's face that she knows; he has no idea how she knows, or how much, but simply that she does. 'Why is it so important to you?' he asks finally, admitting nothing.

'It's important to Jazz,' she says. 'Please, Hari, tell me, for his sake.'

Hassan sighs, and she follows his gaze down to their intertwined hands, hers so vital, the pulse throbbing intimately against his palm, and his so withered and bloodless. Aruna doesn't let go, hoping that her touch, her connection to him, will persuade him to confide. She half-holds her breath while she waits for his decision, and when he starts to speak lets out a gentle exhalation. 'I married her because she was my friend's cousin, and because she'd got herself in trouble. I wanted to help her. She never told me who his real father was. I never asked. It didn't matter to me; I was Jazz's real father in every sense that matters,' he says. A slight coughing fit takes him over, and his chest rattles for a moment, and then he says, 'After all, he couldn't hate his real father any more than he hates me.'

'I don't think he hates you,' says Aruna, 'but I know that perhaps he doesn't understand everything.'

'Oh, he hates me,' says Hassan, 'of course he does. Why else does he keep me here like this? He wants me to live out every miserable moment of my miserable life trapped in a rotting, failing body.' He turns towards her, and says frankly, 'I told you I dream of heart attacks. I dream of strokes. I dream of the ultimate, beautiful solution of suicide, carried out in dozens of painless ways. But you guessed that already.'

Aruna had once seen a man attempt suicide. She and Patrick had gone on holiday to France for Christmas and New Year, escaping his family, and stayed at an exquisite hotel on the south-west coast at Biarritz. On Christmas Day Aruna had woken up to find Patrick nuzzling against her with gratifying enthusiasm, pulling down their blankets, which were surprisingly scratchy for such an expensive hotel, uncovering her body inch by inch. 'Do you mind if I unwrap my Christmas present now?' he teased, kissing her neck, her shoulders and her small breasts as they emerged from the snowy sheets.

'As long as I get mine at the same time,' said Aruna,

218

wrapping her arms around him. 'Mmm, you smell good enough to eat,' she added.

'Did you just pay me a compliment?' said Patrick, lifting his head in surprise. 'Do that again, I like it.' Aruna looked at him blankly, and he asked a little impatiently, a note of amused annoyance in his voice, 'Really Aruna? Can you really not think of anything else to say?'

'Give me a moment,' said Aruna, and a few seconds later announced triumphantly, 'I've got one! You sound fantastically sexy when you speak French.' She had never heard Patrick speak a foreign language before this trip, and although she couldn't speak or understand French at all, he seemed terribly appealing when he did.

'*Vraiment, ma petite cherie*?' he replied jokily, with the surprisingly convincing accent he had acquired during a much-resented teenage year in Belgium. 'Anything else, or am I pushing it here?'

Aruna shut her eyes, and feeling his warm flesh against her, realized that she had an opportunity to be kind; she allowed herself to sink into the seductive softness of intimacy, but only for a moment, in case she got caught there and couldn't claw her way out. She put her hands on either side of his face, her fingers trailing into his hazel curls, and gazed straight at him, for once without him asking her to. 'You have extremely beautiful eyes,' she said with an appreciation so sincere there wasn't an ounce of flirtation to it.

'You're amazing,' he murmured in response. He said it again an hour later, but then they had the Fight About Being Aloof, about her pushing him away when they got too close, about her not saying she loved him, and he walked out of the hotel in a temper, on the day that Aruna had tried, in her own way, to show that she might care.

Later, in an uneasy truce, they walked along the beach. It was cold but the sunshine was brilliant, and the sea alive with heaving, muscular waves as it pounded against the rocks. 'I feel so small when I see the sea,' said Patrick at last, holding her hand as they walked along, as he always did, even when he was cross with her. 'It makes me think of everything in the world that I'll never know, never experience. There's a vast ocean out there, and all that I can take is a pebble from the beach.'

'Do you feel that you've not seen enough?' asked Aruna. She was uncomfortably aware that sometimes she felt that she'd seen too much of the ocean's vastness; that she was like driftwood, floating between two worlds, swinging between her two poles, and no longer sure that either the place she came from, or the place she was going to, was where she belonged.

'I used to think I hadn't seen enough,' said Patrick, 'but then you came along, and I realized that I knew everything about the world that I needed to know, just by holding your hand. That I didn't need to go to the world, because it had come to me.'

'God, you are a romantic, aren't you?' said Aruna, touched despite herself. She glanced up at his face, and saw that he was no longer angry with her, that the last traces of their argument had disappeared like smoke over the waves, just leaving him a little pensive, a little sad. She knew that she had hurt him that morning, with what she had said, with what she had refused to say, and yet he loved her no less; she felt the inexplicable guilt of someone who has got away with something, who has got their own way more times than they deserved. She suspected that the worse the imbalance got between them, the harder the inevitable reckoning would be.

He squeezed her hand, and stopped walking, still looking out to sea. 'You know, before you turned up I used to think that I was ordinary. An ordinary bloke, allright looking, who lived for his job, played rugby on Saturdays and who remembered to floss his teeth. But then I met you, and I began to believe that I was more than ordinary, that I might be extraordinary, after all. I had to be, because you wanted me, because you saw something in me that I didn't even know I possessed. If there's anything slightly special about me, it's because of you.'

Aruna was silent at this confession, and almost humbled at how selfish she had been, assuming that all the insecurity in their relationship belonged to her. She had always guiltily liked being mistaken for the person that

Patrick thought she was; it had never occurred to her that he might feel the same way, that he liked being the heroic, intensely desirable person, as solid as rock, that she had always seen, but that he himself had thought he was someone less than this. She found it hard to believe that her perception of him wasn't the truer one, even though she knew it would have been ridiculous to claim out loud that she knew better who he really was. Patrick didn't seem to mind that she hadn't said anything; he put his arm around her, and they carried on walking, and came to Port Vieux, looking down over its cliff-lined bay, where a few people were lying on the sand and sunning themselves as though it was still summer. There was even someone in the water. 'He's brave,' commented Aruna. 'It's really choppy out there. And probably freezing.'

'Stupid, more like,' said Patrick, 'Or suicidal,' he added, glancing over at the bobbing body. He stopped and stared properly at the swimmer, and Aruna, following his gaze, realized that the man was fully dressed in the water, he wasn't a casual bather after all. 'Christ, he's turned face down,' Patrick cried out, and ran down the wide steps towards the beach, shouting to the people there to call for help. Aruna ran after him, and caught him up by the water's edge. 'He's too far out to get back safely,' said Patrick. 'They're calling for helicopter rescue.' They waited one agonizing minute, with everyone staring at the rolling body in the same helpless way, a dark shadow in the sparkling, sunlit sea like a smudge on a holiday photo. 'It's not going to get here in time, is it?'

said Patrick matter-of-factly, and pulling off his jacket, he ran into the sea. He disappeared immediately under the heaving waves, and Aruna realized how easy it must have been for the drowning man to walk into the water without anyone noticing; one moment there might have been a figure contemplating the vastness of the ocean, and in less than a blink of an eye, there would have been no one there at all, as though he had only been a trick of the light in the first place.

'*Il est fou, l'Anglais*,' said one man to Aruna; seeing she didn't understand, he added in thickly accented English, 'that man, he is mad. He could drown trying to save a suicide.'

'He's my husband,' she said shortly, unsure why it was so important to her that she announce this, ignoring the dark side of her that pointed out it would have been much easier to agree with the man, to nod disloyally, 'Yes, he is mad,' and to watch the scene with the detachment of a passer-by. She supposed she felt responsible for Patrick's act of madness, and this responsibility made her feel both proud and defensive; she wondered if it was possible that he might have leapt bravely into the sea to live up to her expectations of him.

After a few short minutes, that seemed to move in slow motion to Aruna as she saw Patrick's broad back sink completely and then re-emerge between the violent waves, he came back out of the water, dripping and shivering, and dragging the man behind him. A cheer went up from the gathering crowd, which Patrick ignored; he simply announced himself as '*médécin*' as he checked for vital signs and performed CPR until the helicopter arrived with paramedics. The man was strapped up and loaded into the helicopter and sailed off into the sky. The locals patted Patrick on the back, offering him towels and dry clothes, while Aruna stood by his side. She didn't feel relief, as she had surprisingly felt no fear for him; with a belief in his physical ability so extreme that it was wholly irrational, she had been certain that he would succeed. Instead, she found herself thinking only of the man that he had saved, of the desperately sad look in his eyes, that he had not only failed in his life, he had even failed in his death. She wondered if there were many better ways to go, than in the sparkling sea on Christmas Day, in the white light of a beautiful beach full of sunbathers, who would ignore you conveniently, as you strode in to let the churning water massage away your life.

'Are you sure you don't want my kids?' said Patrick, getting into a hot bath back at the hotel, 'I'm a hero, apparently.'

'Yes, you are,' said Aruna flatly.

'You're mad with me for going in, aren't you?' he said. 'I didn't mean to upset you, but he'd have died otherwise. And no one else was going to do it. I wouldn't have gone in if I thought I wouldn't have made it.'

'You were very brave,' agreed Aruna, 'but yes, I am mad with you for going in.' She saw Patrick glow with the heat of the bath and with pleasure at her concern, but in fact she was more angry on behalf of the man he'd pulled from the water. She went out onto the balcony to smoke, and tried to imagine what it must have been like, to have had a glimpse of heaven, to have touched the face of God, and then been dragged back like a sack of potatoes over dry land, strapped into a collapsible bed and imprisoned in a hospital.

'Do you think you could ask Jazz to come in and speak to me?' says Hassan, 'Persuade him, I mean. It's important.'

'Yes,' says Aruna, with gentle pressure on his fragile hand. 'Yes, I can.'

Hassan

Kuala Lumpur General Hospital, Malaysia

Hari Hassan sits upright in his hospital bed, waiting for his son. Part of him is unsure whether he will see him, after all, but because he is still human, albeit barely, he hopes, even when he knows that hope changes nothing. And then, without even a knock on the door, Jazz pushes his way urgently into the room, and stops short, looking horrified at the sight of him. 'Hello Baba,' he says inadequately.

'Hello Ejazzy-Jazz,' says Hassan, his voice breaking into a sob as he realizes that, for once, his hopes have been fulfilled. Come home, my darling, darling child. I've waited so long.

'Why didn't you tell me, Baba? That you weren't my father, that you married Amma to look after her?' Jazz asks reproachfully, 'Rooney's told me everything.'

'I made a promise to your mother,' says Hassan simply. 'She was afraid of what you'd think of her if the truth came out.'

226

'I didn't understand,' says Jazz, lost between remorse and frustration. 'When you told me that you had never loved Amma, when you told me that she always knew that and understood. It's why I've been so angry with you. I thought she killed herself because you weren't there for her. Sometimes I wondered whether you helped her on her way. It's why I abandoned you in this place after the diagnosis.' He sits by the bed, his head sinking into his hands, his entire prone body an expression of distress. 'All those letters you wrote and you never told me.'

'It wasn't my secret, son. I'm sure that your mother wouldn't want me to tell you even now, but the sad fact is that I am too worn out and transparent to hide secrets any more. I'm a selfish old man, and I don't want to die being hated by my only child.'

Jazz looks up, and asks simply, 'So, tell me the truth, Baba. If you're not keeping secrets any more. Was Amma's death an accident?'

Hassan shakes his head, 'I never knew for certain, until today. I've always felt responsible because I wasn't there the day it happened. But I don't think it would have made a difference; it would have just happened another time.' He reaches painfully for and passes over Anwar's letter. 'Please don't judge your mother, Jazz. She loved you so much. You were her world; she didn't want you to have to see her in pain.' Jazz reads the letter, and starts sobbing uncontrollably, burying his face against his father's dead legs, and crushing the paper in his fist as he pounds the bed; Hassan sits helplessly, his parchment-pure hand stroking his son's hair. He still doesn't believe that it's not his blood running in this young man's veins, that the salt and sunshine scent of Jazz's skin doesn't belong to him. 'You have always been mine,' he murmurs, as much to himself as to Jazz, 'I never for a moment felt you weren't.'

Jazz pushes himself up from the bed, and as he calms down, says quietly, 'I know now what you meant, when you wrote that we need to forgive each other. I never knew what it was that you had to forgive me for. I'm so sorry, Baba.'

Hassan reaches out to Jazz, to hold his hand with as much strength as he can muster. 'I'm sorry too, Jazz. I wish I had been a better father, a better husband. I wish that your mother and I had told you the truth. But you will never know the absolute joy that you brought to my life; I have always loved you. I always will love you.' Hassan looks at his son's face, and feels a peace descend on him that he hasn't felt for a long time; he knows he has been forgiven, after all.

'What can I do for you, now, Baba?' Jazz asks at last. 'Is there anything you need from me? To make you more comfortable here.'

'Yes,' says Hassan. He looks with untempered affection at Jazz's face. 'I do need something from you, my son.' He breathes deeply, and says slowly and deliberately, so there can be no possible misunderstanding of his words, 'Jazz, I need you to let me go.'

Jazz stares at his father, his face beginning to crumple

as he realizes what he means. 'But you might live for months, Baba,' he stammers with emotion, 'you might live for years. It might not get any worse. Or they might find some way to arrest the disease, reverse it even.'

'A magic cure?' says Hassan ruefully at his son's arguments. 'I'm not like you, Jazz. I don't believe in magic, or miracles.' He adds with a smile, 'Although I can't tell you how happy I am that you still do.'

When Jazz was three years old, Hassan had taken him and his mother to a hotel in an elegant part of London, near Berkeley Square. Hassan had taught Jazz that classic old song about the nightingales that sang there, and foolishly offered to help him look for them; he was completely unprepared for how distressed his little boy would be, to find out that there really weren't any nightingales after all. He couldn't bear to be responsible for Jazz's infant disappointment, and so he wasted a whole afternoon and morning making enquiries among the specialist shops in Mayfair, before he finally tracked down a pair of bejewelled mechanical nightingales, and bought them at vast expense. He carefully set them up on a tree in the manicured green of Berkeley Square the day after that disappointing first visit. 'So much trouble and money for such a little boy,' Zaida had said about his plan. 'You'll spoil him.' But her tone was that of tender exasperation, rather than disapproval.

Hassan brought Jazz back to Berkeley Square, and wound the nightingales up while his son was distracted with his ball; and then, like magic, the birds began to sing, and flapped with clockwork stiffness in time to the melody. Jazz was so overexcited by the discovery that he ran right into the tree, almost dislodging them. 'We finded them, Baba!' he squealed with excitement. 'We finded the nite-nite-gales!' From then on, Jazz had always claimed that he believed in magic. And miracles. And Hassan had never disappointed him by telling him otherwise; that the nite-nite-gales had been nothing more or less magical and miraculous than the impractical desire of an ageing man to delight his toddling son.

Hassan, looking at grown-up Jazz now, can still see the determined optimism that he had as a child. He wishes, for his son's sake, that there might be another extravagant gesture that he could make that would avoid disappointing him once more. But this time there is nothing he can do. 'I can't fight this disease, Jazz,' he says gently. 'We both know that it's already won. This is all I have to ask of you now.' He breathes deeply, and says once more, realizing that he is begging, 'Please, Jazz. I need you to let me go.'

Jazz seems unable to say anything for a long time, but then he nods silently, and puts his arms around his father's frail form, holding him tight. He doesn't let go, but listens intently as Hassan tells him what he needs to be done. Jazz kisses his father's forehead, and remains by his side, until Nurse eventually returns to prepare him for sleep.

Jazz

Kuala Lumpur General Hospital, Malaysia

Jazz stumbles out of his father's room, but doesn't make it too far before he collapses on the floor, and sits there, his back to the wall, unable to move. He is so wrung out that he can no longer cry, and instead enormous dry sobs heave his whole body so much that he feels he might retch. He has just found his father again after two years, and he isn't ready to let him go, after all. It feels like he has lost him twice. I can't expect him to go on living for me, Jazz keeps repeating to himself, and pulling himself together, he prepares to carry out his dying father's wishes, a last act of love, and duty. He goes to the hospital administrator, and formally removes his objection to the Do Not Resuscitate paperwork. Then, hesitating just for a moment, he finds the room where his father had told him they were playing *Thelma and Louise*, and gives a student volunteer a note from his father, requesting that they send some popcorn up to his room, as a treat. At least I got the chance to say goodbye, Jazz thinks to himself, already bereaved. He goes to where Aruna has been waiting for him, and tells her what he has just done, afraid of accusation, hoping for absolution. She puts her arms around him, and they walk away from the hospital, clinging to each other; he is aware that he is staggering slightly, like a survivor of a war.

'It's all he wanted from you,' says Aruna quietly, as he stands and looks back at the hospital building looming out of the darkness, like a ship in the night, the lights in the windows glowing steadily. 'To be forgiven, and to be let go. Maybe that's all anyone needs, once they choose to die.' Jazz wonders, as she says this, glancing at her profile lit by the harsh glare of the city street lamps, whether the needs of those who choose to live are so very different.

They take the overnight train back to Singapore, leaving late in the evening and arriving first thing in the morning. On the train, they go over the revelations of the evening again and again. 'Baba didn't know who my real father was,' says Jazz. 'It feels odd that we do. I just can't get over it. Your dad. Really, your dad? If we share a father, he had to have been my dad too. I mean, I knew him, and I never felt a thing for him.'

'I don't think my dad knew about you either; the timing of Zaida's pregnancy might have made him sus-pect, but he probably assumed you were Hari's son. Not many people would have taken on a wife who was carrying someone else's child, at least in those days. Your dad was pretty special,' says Aruna.

'What's completely freaking me out is that Amma must have known,' mutters Jazz. 'She knew all along that you were my half-sister, and she never said a word.' His mother knew Aruna's dad, and he remembers the way she talked about his personal tragedy, the early death of his young wife. He wonders now whether there had been a shadowy flicker of relief when she told this story, of self-satisfaction even, that her life had worked out after all, and that his, after presumably abandoning her after a brief affair to go back to his pregnant wife, had not. And his Amma had always been so kind to motherless Aruna, insisting she call her Auntie, fixing her hair, baking her cookies, treating her like she really was the sister that Jazz had never had. Perhaps this knowledge was so entrenched in his mother, the fact of their shared blood, the natural inevitability of their close bond, that it never really occurred to her, that one day he and Aruna might become more than good friends. It seems so naive, but he supposes his mother was quite naive, in some ways; she had gone straight from her parents' house to her husband's house, by means of an ill-advised liaison with a married man visiting from Singapore; she had never worked, and knew less about the world than he might have supposed. When she left Singapore to return to Kuala Lumpur, she had still considered Jazz and Aruna to be children. Perhaps she really thought that they would remain children forever.

'What matters is that we know now, Jazz,' says Aruna. 'At least we finally know what we are to each other.'

'Do we?' asks Jazz, looking out into the black, sticky night as the train rumbles on the track.

When Jazz and Aruna were in their first year of school, they would sit in the corner of the playground, cross-legged, knees touching, and talk, and talk, and talk. They would work on their porn-star names, using the name of their first pet (neither of them had a first pet as yet, and so they had infinite choice), and their mother's maiden name. 'Ruffles Kamran' was Jazz's favourite, who hoped to have a dog one day, and 'Goldie Ullah' was Aruna's, who more practically expected to get a goldfish. They would ask questions, like, 'If you were in a jungle, what would you see?' Aruna would say, 'Trees and tigers and snakes,' and Jazz would say, 'Tarzan,' and make the whoo-hooing jungle call, beating his chest like a gorilla to make her laugh.

'What would you do if you were in a wilderness, and you came across a huge lake?' Aruna asked one lunch-time recreation. She claimed that she would dive in and swim, but Jazz didn't believe her.

'You'd be worried about the lurgies, beasties and

bugs,' he said. 'And infectious diseases in the water. And having to walk around in damp clothes afterwards.'

'I'm not as wimpy and helpless as you think,' she pointed out mulishly, lifting her chin to make the point. 'I'd totally dive right in and swim across to the other side. Besides, it's my lake, so it would be a gorgeous one, surrounded by beautiful trees with clear, warm water that reflected the sky, and maybe a few trailing reeds.' She asked him again, 'So what would you do?'

'I'd just walk around it,' admitted Jazz. 'What do you think that means?'

'That you're an avoider,' suggested Aruna, a bit smugly, 'and I'm not.' She squealed as he started throwing his crisps at her.

'Try not avoiding these.' He laughed, and emptied the packet over her head with a flourish.

'God, you're such a *boy*,' she complained, as though this was the worst insult she could think of. 'I'm telling your mum you did that. Look, you utter moron, I've got salt and cruddy flakes all over my hair.'

'God, you're such a *girl*,' Jazz retorted. 'It'll wash out, anyway.'

'It's itchy,' Aruna muttered. 'You're so gross.'

Jazz shrugged. 'Can I share your peanuts? I've lost all my crisps,' he asked.

'Are you kidding me? No!' said Aruna.

'Please-please-pretty-please-with-sugar-and-a-cherry-on-top and Amma's making cookies if you want to come back after school,' wheedled Jazz.

'Oh, go on then,' said Aruna, passing him her peanuts. 'And don't beg, it's not dignified.' She waited a second, and then said swiftly, 'Bagsy on licking out the bowl.'

'Like that's dignified,' complained Jazz, secretly annoyed he hadn't thought of it first.

Jazz looks at Aruna, who is trying to sleep against the stiff-backed bench of the train, and when he catches her eye, he says unthinkingly, 'Goldie Ullah.'

'Ruffles Kamran,' she replies instinctively, grinning at how she doesn't even need to remember.

Jazz smiles, and says, 'We were more than a couple, Rooney. More than lovers. We were friends first. That's what I missed most when you went away. I missed my best friend. What we found out today doesn't change that; you know I'll always be here for you.'

'Nearness in birth or blood doth but persuade a nearer nearness in affection,' says Aruna thoughtfully.

'What's that meant to mean?' says Jazz, who no longer remembered the quote from the Ford play, having put it deliberately from his mind after that day.

'It means, I know,' says Aruna. 'It means, me too.' She shuffles over to sit beside him, and rests her head lightly on his shoulder. He puts his arm around her, and completely comfortable and settled into each other, they both manage to fall asleep to the rumble of the train and the mild scent of damp and fuel.

Aruna

Singapore Train Station

Aruna stirs with the early morning light, just before they come back into Singapore. Two days ago, she didn't think she would ever wake up with Jazz again, and now as she wakes in his arms, her head nestled against his neck, she is surprised at how normal it still feels, there is nothing controversial, no niggle of disquiet or discomfort, it feels the most natural thing in the world. Her brother enemy. Her brother friend. She finally has the answer she wanted, she is finally going home; she should feel satisfied, or at least content, but instead she feels ambiguous. Instead of feeling full of hope for the future, she is instead thinking only of the recent past. She is thinking that it is late evening back in London, and that Patrick is going to sleep in a flat that is still empty. She is thinking of what she left behind in the other place that she never allowed herself to call home. Like driftwood, she thinks, floating between two worlds.

'I just wish you'd tell me why,' Patrick said, at home one evening after work, slicing courgettes for the pasta sauce.

'Sorry, I've got some work to do,' said Aruna, not sounding nearly sorry enough, and she unplugged her laptop and went to the bedroom.

Patrick put down the knife, turned off his simmering pots, and simply followed her. 'I mean, is it because my mum said I was a ten-pound baby? Because I'm not sure that's true.'

'Of course it's true,' said Aruna, instantly annoyed with herself that she'd let him draw her back into the conversation. 'Just look at the size of you. But it's not that.'

'Is it because of how your mum died? Because that wouldn't happen to you, there's better monitoring of that sort of thing these days.'

'No,' said Aruna shortly.

'Is it because you think I won't make love to you when you're pregnant? Because that's really not a problem. I'll just be careful; if you're careful too, we can make love right up to the end.'

'Reassuring that you don't mind making love to a Zeppelin, but it's not that,' muttered Aruna. 'I'm getting really tired of having this conversation, you know; you've not let up since we got back from France. Every time you come in from work, it's like the blade jabbing behind the shower curtain in *Psycho*, "Baby, baby, baby", to the tune of shrieking violins.'

'Is it because you'd have to stop drinking and smoking, and anything else you take on the side, when I'm not about?' Patrick persisted. 'Because we can get help with that. If you think it would be a problem giving them up.'

Aruna finally lost her temper. 'I don't need your fucking help, Patrick,' she shouted. 'I don't need help. And I don't need your babies. Now get the hell out of here!'

'No!' Patrick shouted back, slamming the bedroom door behind him with a violence that surprised both of them. 'Not this time. For once in your life have enough fucking respect for me to tell me what's going on with you. I want you to talk to me. I want you to tell me the truth.'

Aruna laughed hysterically, as she felt herself snap, and her tentative self-control careered wildly away. 'You really want to know the truth? The truth is that I got pregnant three times with my ex-boyfriend, and miscarried them all. The truth is that you married the dead-baby machine, so if all you want is kids from me you'd better find someone else.'

Patrick's fight seeped out of him, and he sank down on the bed in shock. Aruna's bitter confession clearly wasn't the truth he'd been expecting. 'Christ, Aruna. Three miscarriages. Why didn't you tell me before? We need to talk about these sorts of things, you shouldn't try and deal with this stuff on your own.' He looked up and saw Aruna was still trembling and pale with fury. 'How long were you with your ex-boyfriend, to have had three miscarriages?' he asked.

'Twenty-odd years, give or take,' she said bluntly, 'since we were ten years old. We were at school together.'

'You've been with someone for twenty years, and you

never mentioned him to me,' said Patrick, astounded. 'You don't trust me enough to tell me a thing, do you? You don't want me to know anything about you.' He hesitated, then asked, 'Is that why you broke up with him and came here? Because of the miscarriages?'

Aruna shook her head, 'He just . . . wasn't available to me any more,' she said. 'I don't want to talk about this, it's personal.'

'You're right, it is,' said Patrick, 'which is why we need to talk about it. I mean, what does "wasn't available" mean? Did he turn out to be gay? Did he get married? Fall into a coma?' He paused and asked, 'Did he betray you, let you down, I mean?'

'I suppose you could say that I let him down,' replied Aruna, 'but not in the way you mean.'

'So, what happened?' asked Patrick.

'I just left,' she said. 'Left him, left Singapore. I had to. He still doesn't know where I am.'

Patrick stared at her with an expression approaching disgust, which didn't suit his blunt good looks, it twisted his face into plainness. 'You just left? God, you really are a bitch, Aruna. Is that what you do to people you love? Just leave?'

Aruna stepped over and slapped him hard across the face, 'You know nothing about it,' she hissed. 'Don't you dare judge me. You have no idea how much I loved him.'

'You're right. I don't. I have no idea whether you even love me, when it comes down to it. You've never said the words. Not ever,' he shouted back.

'I can't take any more of this, I'm leaving,' she spat out, and went to open the door, but Patrick took her arm and yanked her back into the room.

'Not this time,' he yelled. 'You're not just walking out again – you're going to talk to me this time. We're finishing this.'

'Just let me out, you freak,' she screamed with impotent fury at being so easily manhandled, and picking up the bedside lamp she threw it at him viciously and went for the door again. The lamp smashed harmlessly on the floor behind Patrick, and he caught her and slammed her back bodily against the wall to stop her. And then everything went black as she cracked her head and passed out.

Aruna came blearily to consciousness to find herself in Patrick's arms while he sat on the floor; he was rocking her against him, and crying helplessly like a lost child. 'I'm so sorry, darling, I'm so sorry. Please don't leave me. Please don't leave me,' he kept saying. 'I didn't mean it, I didn't want to hurt you, I just wanted to stop you from going. I was angry, I didn't mean to push so hard. Please don't leave me.' Aruna realized fuzzily through the pain that it was oddly poignant to see such a big man so broken down.

'I know you didn't mean it,' she said. 'I'm sorry, too.'

'You shouldn't be sorry,' Patrick said, tears still running freely down his cheeks, 'You tell me about this awful thing that's happened to you, and I just act like a freak, like you said, because you mentioned your ex-boyfriend. I know you keep saying that I'm not jealous, but the truth is I am. I'm jealous of your past; I'm jealous of before you met me. I don't know a thing about your life before you came to London. I'm jealous of all the things I know you don't want to tell me.'

Aruna pulled herself out of his embrace, and moved awkwardly away from him, to lean with her back against the side of their bed. 'I'm sorry because I've done this to you,' she said. 'I've taken the kindest, gentlest man I know, and turned him into someone who slams his wife against the wall during a quarrel. I've made you ugly. And angry. And I'm sorry.' Her head was throbbing, and she felt bruised and sore down one side of her, especially across her hip bone; she crawled onto the bed, and lay down on top of the covers, with her face up as she fingered the sore lump under the hair.

Patrick leaned across, and brushed his hand across the tender patch. 'Let me get you some ice for that, to help with the swelling,' he said. He ran to the kitchen, and came back with the tray of ice cubes, efficiently emptying the ice into a plastic bag, which he held against her head. He pressed his cheek against her limp hand on the bed, and said again, 'I'm so sorry I hurt you.'

'I hurt you all the time, and you just sit there and take it,' she said frankly. For some reason she felt saner than she had in days, the crack to her head seemed to be focusing all her mental energy on the pain, rather than in mixing her up.

'You don't hurt me, really. I know you say hurtful things, sometimes, but I also know you don't mean them,' said Patrick. 'That's something I've known for a long time.' He paused, looking carefully at her face, as though he wanted to say something more, or was hoping for her to say something in response; for a moment the silence was full of the things unsaid between them. The pain in Aruna's head was sharpening to something white hot and overwhelming. She closed her eyes.

He sat with her for a while, gently tracing her jawbone with the side of his palm, and then eventually he said, 'I need to tell you something. I didn't mean what I said just now, either. I want you to know, that I do know you love me. Of course I'd like you to say it, just occasionally, but the thing is, you don't have to say it for me to know. I see it in all the little things you do, in the way you always leave your hand out of your pocket when we're walking down the street for me to take, in the way you make those funny side comments and wait to see if I'll laugh, in the way you hold me in your arms as though you'll never let me go, in the way you make love to me like there's never been anyone else. I know you love me. If I died in a car crash tomorrow, I'd die knowing that you loved me; you'd never have to regret not having said it.'

Somehow, the tone of his tender words, soaked in so much undiluted emotion and belief, hurt Aruna more than her head; she wished so much that she could be the person he thought her to be, that she burst into tears and found she really couldn't stop. Patrick moved beside her onto the bed, and took her in his arms again, and just held her as she cried.

In the middle of the night, Aruna slid out of Patrick's sleeping embrace, pulled her enormous dressing gown over her bruised body, and went to sit on their garden step as she smoked. She thought about Jazz, whom she had loved and abandoned without a word, because he was no longer available to her; and Patrick, whom she had damaged and wasn't sure she could love, because she wasn't available to him either, because she was still filled with the past and always drifting back to her other world, her previous existence. She wondered how many other people she would hurt incontrovertibly in her life, because of the swinging pendulum in her head that told her sometimes she would be very, very good, and sometimes that she would be horrid. She could run away, but she couldn't escape, and she couldn't move on. I'm a horrible, horrible person, she thought to herself, I wasn't always that way, but I've become one. The voices in her head that the medication used to muffle, argued that the world might be a pleasanter place without her, and she wasn't able to disagree.

The next day, Aruna left a note for Patrick, apologizing for everything, again. She apologized for the mess, the one she had left in the kitchen, and the one she had left in his life. She tried to explain that she knew he had been a good husband, and that her unhappiness had nothing to do with him; that in fact, she truly wished she could have allowed herself to accept and return his love, to have been happy for his sake, and have made him happy too. She packed a bag with swimming gear, and went to the Hampstead Heath Ponds, to the lake fringed by beautiful trees, which reflected the sky, with reeds swaying just under the surface. It wasn't as easy for her as it should have been for the man in Biarritz; she dived, and just came back bobbing to the surface. She couldn't put stones in her pockets, as she had no pockets, and there were no stones. Defeated by the calm stillness of the ponds, by the beauty of the surroundings, by the curious looks of the local pensioners placidly bathing at the chilly water's edge in unflattering patterned swimwear with scalps squeezed under scalloped rubber caps, she left the water, got dressed, and went back to their flat. She told herself, told the voices if they were there to listen, that it would be more considerate to everyone if she tried to live. And so her life went on after all; in the weeks and months that followed, she and Patrick continued to make love often and with enthusiasm, they continued to bicker, she continued to reject her medication and self-medicate instead with drink and hash, she continued her academic work and research, and she continued to refuse to discuss the possibility of having a child. Everything continued, until a few days before her first wedding anniversary, when she read a line in a book over breakfast, and then everything changed with the drama of lights dying in a theatre, and a curtain rising to show a different world displayed on a shining stage.

Aruna looks over at Jazz, still sleeping. She takes her medication out of her handbag, and stares at the nonde-script bottle, the plain label marked with her name; she remembers how she had once thought she would rather be dead than half-alive. She shakes the bottle experimen-tally, and with the slight rattle, Jazz stirs beside her; before she can change her mind, she unscrews the top and takes her pills, and then replaces the bottle guiltily as though she has done something she shouldn't have. It's better to live, she tells herself, it's better to have even half a life, to have half a chance for happiness, than none at all. She nudges Jazz gently with her elbow as the train pulls into the station, 'Wake up,' she says, 'We're back.'

Hassan

Kuala Lumpur General Hospital, Malaysia

Hassan wakes later than usual in the hospital; he wonders if his son has made it home yet. He is feeling no fear, no trepidation today and no nostalgia for his long journey; he just feels a vast relief, like a runner coming in for the final lap, just seeking the end. His floating world has spun full circle in just a couple of days, and has finally been tethered in place; he has been forgiven by his son, and forgiven in his turn, his conscience over his poor wife has been cleared, and he has seen Aruna's swimmable, drown-innable eyes. He does not seriously believe that Aruna might be his missing daughter's child, as he believes in neither magic nor miracles, but he likes the idea that it might be possible, however remotely. Seeing Aruna has given him hope that something of Nazneen might have survived after all. He likes his world today; he sees the world as a good place, full of good people, with ordinary cares, performing everyday kindnesses. Nurse comes in, the practical Malay one that he likes,

248

and with a crisp, '*Selamat pagi*,' ministers to him effi-ciently.

'Don't worry, Nurse,' he says with an uncharacteristic smile. 'I'm not planning to die on your shift. I wouldn't dare.'

'*Maaf?*' asks Nurse in confusion, 'Pardon?' as her firm and efficient exterior ripples for a moment like a pool.

'*Maafkan saya*,' says Hassan, 'Excuse me. I'm just a bit confused today. Too many visitors yesterday.'

'Well, hopefully you'll have no visitors today, then,' says Nurse, recovering herself briskly, as though embar-rassed by her momentary lapse.

She leaves the room, and Hassan reaches under his pillowcase to touch his hidden stash of popcorn, and feels an extraordinary delight, like a child who has received a visit from the tooth fairy, or found a chocolate egg hid-den in the garden. Nurse will be off duty this evening, he thinks with satisfaction, and every minute is bringing him closer. He hopes that Jazz won't have too much trouble sorting out the house, and his possessions; Hassan feels a slight embarrassment at the amount of things he has accumulated over the years, ridiculous when he knew that they were never going to come with him, that in the end he would leave as unburdened as he arrived. He should have told Jazz just to torch the lot and have done with it. At least then Jazz would never find that pair of mechanical nightingales, tucked away in a box in the basement. Those rusty old birds were possibly Hassan's most treasured possession.

Hassan still, however, has one other possession that he values, and this is the one in his hand – he smooths out Anwar's letter over his sheets, and looks at the blank space that follows his final sentence. He wonders what it was his friend was planning to say, that he never had the nerve to write. He wonders whether soon he might be able to ask him himself.

Jazz

Little India, Singapore

'It's weird to see the apartment, again,' says Aruna, looking around at the space that must seem both familiar and strange. Jazz wonders what she is thinking, as she casually picks up the takeaway menus on the kitchen counter that they used to rely on excessively; he has only recently started to cook for himself, which impresses June, as she can't cook at all. He sees Aruna glance with a slightly baffled look at June's porcelain containers of 'Spring in a Bowl' and 'Fields of Freshness' potpourri; surely guessing that they are nothing to do with him. There are photos of him and June stuck to the fridge door with magnets, which Aruna studies with a rueful smile, as though she might think that compared to beautiful, youthful June, she has somehow let herself go. 'Thanks for coming up with me,' says Jazz, 'I've got what I needed now. I'll give you a lift home.'

'I don't need you to do things for me any more,' says Aruna, 'I can do things by myself from now on.'

251

'I know,' says Jazz, 'but this is one thing I want to do for you. So let me.'

In the car, it quickly becomes obvious that Jazz isn't driving her back to her apartment in Holland Village after all. 'Where are we going?' she asks, confused.

'You'll see in a minute,' says Jazz, and a little while later he takes the turning for Changi Airport. Aruna looks at Jazz, stunned, but doesn't say anything further until he pulls up at the terminal building.

'What are we doing here, Jazz?' she asks quietly, as they both get out.

'You know why we're here, Rooney,' says Jazz. 'You didn't come back to Singapore to come home, and you didn't come back for me. You came back to ask me to forgive you for leaving, and to let you go. To say goodbye because we never had the chance to do it before. To finish our story.' Aruna looks like she's about to argue with him, but he doesn't let her. 'And that's what I'm doing, for both of us. I wouldn't change a moment that we shared together, and you will always be my best friend, but now I'm letting you go. And saying goodbye. And saying that you don't need me to forgive you, because I love you; I always have, and I always will.'

Aruna doesn't argue after all, and her eyes fill with tears, 'I don't know, Jazz. I don't know what I'm meant to do now.'

Jazz pulls her into his arms, and hugs her closely, 'I do. I know you too well. I knew that you were never going to stay; you brought your phone with you, Rooney. You never took off your wedding ring.' He strokes her hair, and says, 'I'm just telling you what you already know. On the other side of the world, there's someone who loves you. The rest is up to you.'

Aruna says nothing; she seems so weak-limbed in his arms that he is practically holding her up. 'How should a story finish, Jazz?' she asks at last.

Jazz smiles wryly, 'There are lots of good ways to finish a story,' he says. 'With a party, or a birth, or a death, or a disquieting anticlimax.'

'But what's the best way?' she persists, smiling herself now, even with her damp eyes.

'You know that all my stories end the same way.' He shrugs with a little embarrassment, 'With a kiss, and happy ever after.'

'So can that be how we'll end ours?' she asks. And with that simple, final request, Jazz knows that he was right. They lean across, and kiss each other gently, and warmly on the lips. Their happy ever after kiss. Their secret.

'I've got a present before you go,' says Jazz, and he gives her the proof of his latest book, which he has just taken from the apartment. 'I'm sorry it's not very original, to give you another book, but I couldn't think of anything else. We never gave each other presents, did we?'

'Thank you,' says Aruna, looking down at his novel, seeming absurdly touched. She looks at him seriously, and asks, 'You do know how much I love you, don't you?'

Jazz nods. 'Of course I know. You don't need to tell me.' He smooths back her hair from her face, and the tears from her eyes, with a familiar gesture, that is even a little proprietorial, like a parent tidying a child before a school gate. 'Go on, Rooney,' he says. 'Go home. I hope it works out for you. Remember, I believe in happy ever after. I believe in magic. And I believe in you.' He adds with a grin, 'I always have. And I always will.'

He gets back in the car, and sees Aruna take a few hesitant steps towards the terminal building, and then pausing as though still not absolutely sure of what she intends to do. She opens his book, and as she reads the note that he has written to her, scrawled on the inside page in his untidy hand, she turns swiftly to look back at him, smiling again through her tears, almost laughing. I've done it, thinks Jazz, I finally had the strength to give back what I no longer had the right to own. And then he watches her walk away.

Aruna

King Edward's Road, Bethnal Green, London

Aruna gets to the flat just before midnight, and realizes once she is there that she doesn't have her keys, that they are probably still inside on the glass table in the hallway. She stands uncertainly before the heavy front door and then presses the buzzer, wondering if Patrick might be working another double shift, wondering whether she might have to wake the neighbours and spend the night on the landing. 'Is that you?' asks an exhausted voice on the intercom. 'I've been waiting up.'

'It's me,' Aruna says, and there is a pause as the lock clicks open. She goes through the high-ceilinged communal entrance hall, and stands in front of the door to her flat, hesitating for a moment. She is back the day after tomorrow, just as he asked her to be. She doesn't know if Patrick will throw himself weeping on her in trembling fury, or indulgently reproach her for returning so late while he fixes her a drink, or just announce that he's too tired to argue with her and is going to bed. She doesn't

255

know if she will finally be able to give him those words she needs to say, and the words he needs to hear, or whether she will simply say, without explanation, 'For you. I came back for you,' and hope that he understands. She doesn't know when she will be able to tell him her story, which she is guarding as carefully within her as a dove that would be crushed if held too firmly, or which would fly off into the sky if held too lightly. All she knows is that she can only walk back, in the same way that she walked away, just one step at a time. One foot, and then the other. Toe to heel to toe to heel.

'Aruna,' calls Patrick from inside the flat, 'the door's open.' The morning after Patrick threw her against the wall, Aruna had watched him as he made the coffee; he almost couldn't bear to look back at her, at the bruises that he had caused, at the sore way she walked; she saw him, unshaven and suffering, with a tense expression about his eyes and mouth. For once, he wasn't that attractive to her, and she could imagine what he might look like when he was much older, and for some reason, this tugged tenderly at the pit of her stomach. She cared for him terribly just then, enough to pack a bag with swimming gear, and go to a lake with a plan to set them both free.

Aruna feels a draught of cold air sweep across the tops of her feet. She hears the rumble of late-night traffic, the light rain beginning to patter on the creaking sash windows with increasingly persistent force. She can see Jazz sitting at his desk, and looking out at the busy Little India streets, as clearly as if she is there herself, shading his eyes from the sun, with the luminous smile of someone who has never stopped believing in magic. She can see Hari drowning blissfully in the beautiful whiteness of his sheets, the hospital walls receding around him as he gratefully chokes and air stops invading his lungs; she can see him as he catches his glimpse of heaven, as he touches the face of God. She hears Patrick moving through the flat, flicking on the switch in their hallway, pushing the door wide, and now he is standing on the threshold in a pool of electric light, waiting for her.

'The door was open,' he says again. 'Aren't you coming in?'

'There's something I have to tell you,' she starts to say, stepping back from him cautiously. 'I think I should have told you before, I should have told you from the start.'

'Aruna, I know,' says Patrick, surprising her into silence. 'I've known for a long time. I found your prescription slip when I was clearing up one day. And then I realized. I wanted to say something about it, I almost did once, after that terrible fight, but I didn't feel I had the right. I knew you didn't trust me enough to tell me.' He asks once more, less confidently, 'Aren't you coming in?'

Aruna thinks how his tiredness, his uncertainty at this moment, mirrors her own. She remembers the line that Hari wrote in a letter to his friend. The words that took her away. She remembers the note that Jazz wrote for her on the inside page of his novel, which she had read while standing indecisively at Changi Airport. The words that sent her back again.

'Yes,' she says, and walks through the door and turns to face him as he shuts it behind her, suspecting now that she might belong to this place of cold draughts, and traffic noise, and persistent rain, where someone has been waiting up to let her in. It is the place she has chosen to be. 'My dearest Rooney,' Jazz had written, 'my sister, my friend. It's time to stop fighting, and go home.'

Acknowledgements

I owe a great deal to my husband, Phil Richards, for this novel; while I was writing it, I did almost nothing else. I forgot to eat or sleep, and didn't do anything helpful around the house apart from look after our children for a few hours a day. He put up with me inhabiting an imaginary world, and looked after us all.

My cousin, Amir Farooqi, and his family, have shown me and my husband amazing hospitality in Singapore over the years, from when I was a backpacking twenty-year-old. They shared their local knowledge with me, and nurtured my affection for the city, which made it a natural setting for this novel.

Paul and Debbie Roebuck were kind enough to check and correct my use of Bahasa for the scenes set in Debbie's native Malaysia.

My agents, Clare Alexander and Ayesha Karim at Aitken Alexander Associates, my editors, Imogen Taylor and Jennifer Weis, and the teams at Macmillan and St Martin's Press, have my thanks for championing this book on first sight when it was what no one had expected.

My mother, Niluffer Farooki, and my sisters, Preeti

Farooki and Kiron Farooki, have always been great readers and a wonderful support to my work.

And finally, I need to thank my two boys, Jaan and Zaki, aged four and three years old respectively, for inspiring me every day, and for showing enormous patience with a mother who spends such an inordinate amount of time working, or as they put it, 'making things up and writing them down'.

Roopa Farooki is the Ambassador for Relate's Family Counselling Service, a registered charity which provides advice, counselling and workshops to children, parents and families in need of support.

www.relate.org.uk